BOMBED BACK TO THE STONE AGE!

CONTENTS

THE BECOMING
BY ROBERT FORD

THE ONLY SOUNDS WERE A GENTLE wind rustling the leaves and the constant, soothing lullaby of the waves against the shoreline. Even the grackles had quieted in the still, high heat of the evening.

Michael tapped his fingertips against the glass top of the patio table and let out a heavy sigh. His chest ached with hurt, a pulse that rose and fell with the sound of the ocean waves.

"Lie to me." Michael turned to look at Jo and stared into her eyes. "Tell me you love me, and I promise I'll believe whatever you say."

Jo's eyes brimmed with tears as she stared quietly at the ocean's horizon.

He knew she was holding back, as she always did, but then a single tear spilled down her face, and she angrily wiped it away.

"I don't have to lie about it." Jo sniffled, shook her head, then slowly reached down and took off her wedding rings. She studied them in the palm of her hand and then sat them on the glass table top. "But I can't do this anymore."

Jo shrugged. "I care about you…" She sniffled again and then met his gaze. "You need help, Michael, and I can't make you get it. But I can't stand by anymore while you—"

"It's happening, Jo."

"Michael…" Her eyes brimmed with tears again, and she looked skyward. "The world is not coming to an end. There isn't any sort of—"

"It is."

"—great war among the—"

"Then explain the diseases, Jo. The earthquakes and the—"

"Shit happens, Michael!" Jo yelled, and the expression on her face showed that she regretted it immediately. She stood up from the vinyl patio chair and put her hands flat on the table. Jo sighed heavily and spoke in a softer voice. "It's cycles of the world. Tectonic plates and people traveling globally, exposing themselves to new viruses and…"

She shook her head as she let her words fade off. "I can't let you draw me into these delusions of yours and… I'm sorry, I really am." Jo turned away and opened the sliding glass door of the townhouse.

Michael stood up, followed her inside, and slid the door closed behind him.

Jo grabbed her keys from the kitchen counter and walked toward the front door. Her maroon suitcase rested there, off to the side. She paused with her back to him and whispered in a trembling voice. "I'll be at my mom's until I figure out what's next."

"Why can't you remember like I can?"

Her shoulders sank, and Jo shook her head. She grabbed the suitcase handle and opened the front door. "Goodbye, Michael."

The high-pitched shriek of air sirens blasted from the distant north and then again from the west. Another air siren joined, then more, until seven became a chorus.

"Michael…" Jo slowly turned back. Her gaze flicked toward the TV, and she crossed the living room and grabbed the remote. Every channel had the colored bars of the Emergency Broadcast System and a shrill tone.

"What's happening?" Jo looked into Michael's eyes.

"I'm sure it's nothing." He smiled softly.

"Don't do that right now." Jo shook her head, muted the TV, and tossed the remote on the couch.

"You already know what's happening." Michael stepped closer. He wanted to reach for her, put his hand gently against the side of her face, hold her close, and tell her it was okay to give herself over. To become.

"You want to control everything, but that's not how it works," Michael whispered.

Tears spilled down her cheeks again, but she didn't wipe them away this time. Jo suddenly dropped to her knees and screamed in pain. Smoke curled up from her skin, and the air smelled of frying meat. The sigils burned on her flesh—the words of the ancients.

Her arms trembled as she met his gaze. "What's… what's happening to me?"

"You're becoming what you've always been." Michael held out his hand. "Stand and fight with me, Jophiel, the beauty of God."

The floor shook beneath them. Plates rattled in the kitchen cabinets. The framed wedding photo fell from the living room wall, and the glass cracked.

When she slid her hand into his, Michael felt the electric arc between them, and Jo snapped her head back. She trembled and then let out a sharp gasp of breath.

"I… I remember…" Her tears turned to blood, and Jo stared at him with crimson eyes. "I remember everything."

Michael smiled and led her outside. Another heavy rumble shook the ground, and seven missiles shot across the sky one by one, leaving a trail of fire and smoke in their wake. Black clouds churned in the sky like boiling water.

"The fiery dragon had seven heads with seven crowns," Michael whispered. "It's time. It's time to stand beside me and fight."

"I love you," she whispered, and in the reflection of her eyes, Michael saw the smoke trails from the Minuteman missiles.

"I know." As the sigils appeared, Michael's flesh began to burn, blood boiling with fire. He felt the bones in his spine shift and pop, breaking and fusing again as his long-missed wings sprouted from his back. Michael clenched his teeth against the agony.

He closed his eyes and let himself become.

THE SILENT PEAK

BY GRAM HZOFIZIN

DEEP IN UNCIVILIZED SPACE ON A DOOMED PLANET, TWO LOVERS PREPARED FOR AN ILL-FATED QUEST: FOK, THE STAR TALKER, AND THE GUIDE SJU.

The volcanic god Astool spewed flames streaking the sky crimson-grey for the past week. Fok claimed this to be an omen, but the tribe treated his concerns as the superstitions of a youngling. Such things had passed before, they would say in reply. Unsatisfied, the two would seek answers from the silent peak towering above the smokey veil.

Leaving the village was difficult because everyone panicked after the last volley of rock crushed some huts. Sju led Fok to the Baki tree, whose hollowed trunk was a natural canoe they could use to cross the mighty river Yyria. They quickly prepared the boat and launched it into the murky waters. During the crossing, they managed to avoid the feared beast of the depths—the Kilhi.

For the pair, ascending the mountain meant the bite of obsidian shards with every grueling step. They climbed miles to reach the peak and found a sky of twinkling orbs.

They turned to take in a full view; the sky unveiled a sight that chilled them to their bones.

The mortally wounded Neirki battled a cosmic monster of starry void that gnawed at the moon's edges and devoured the celestial body with a ravenous hunger that tore chunks of lunar rock with each terrifying bite.

The moon crumbled after the monster's attack ended. Her wounds bled onto the planet below in a shower of molten boulders that pierced the planet's crust and issued forth waves of magma miles high that rolled across the landscape. In their last seconds, the two lovers kissed and embraced as a landslide buried them deep in the mantle.

LIGHT-YEARS AWAY... the celebrated artist Praxamus operated a remote digger via brush strokes on his canvas. The action ground the moon to dust, and cloaked the planet's atmosphere in a perfect shade of grey—a masterpiece to be admired by his peers.

Praxamus loved his marvelous new creation.

TWILIGHT OF THE VITAPHAGE
BY BRIAN ASMAN

T͟HE D͟AY G͟REW L͟ONG in the tooth, the sky reddening to favor the blood-soaked soil below. Throughout the valley of Vonacax, the screams of men in the thick of their dying echoed off the shale, punctuated by the occasional bellow of a wounded mammoth. The stench of ochre and burning flesh hung heavy in their air.

Astride the ancient mountain's spine stood Primus Ashlok, his aged bones aching from the long day of fighting, apprising the cave. Too much of the day had slipped away from them. He'd hoped to find his quarry before sundown, but the brilliantly-bruised western sky told him it was not to be.

He snapped his fingers. Two simplexes clad in scuffed red leather armor dragged the captive forward.

The man was dying from disease and battle. His eyes were clouded, broken blood vessels announcing the infection running rampant through his body, but his skin had yet to scale. He was not so far gone as the other drudges in the last Vitaphage's slave army.

"What's your name?" Ashlok asked.

"Nonavus Terrilon, in another life. My gift?"

"Soon… Is this the redoubt of the one who would be your master?"

"Yes."

"Then may we meet again amongst the spires of Entilash." Ashlok spun his axe, killing edge spattered with drudge-blood, and severed the captive's neck in one clean slash. The man's head tumbled chin-over-brow, rolling over the edge to find some eventual resting place in the valley below.

"Find his head," Ashlok told the nearest diplex, a one-eyed, bearded specimen. "When he burns, burn him whole," then he turned back to the cave opening, the yawning mouth an open question.

"You think he told the truth?" Paraplex Donalek asked.

Ashlok shot his adjutant an annoyed look. Donalek, a nephew of the Primarch, was a political appointee, unlike Ashlok, who'd joined the common ranks as a boy and rose to command the entire army. To its sorrow, men like Donalek, soft and simpering, seemed to be the future of Mu.

"For all our sakes, I hope so," Ashlok responded.

Donalek pointed at the sky. "But what shall we do? Night falls. Soon, it shall be at the height of its powers."

The others of its kind, Ashlok, and his father's, father's, father had hunted over generations, catching them in daylight while they slumbered and dragging them into the sun to their end.

Now their greatest weapon was all but gone, and every man in the war party--seasoned soldiers all—could be turned against their fathers and mothers, consorts, sons, and daughters.

One choice remained.

"We trap it," Ashlok said. "Ready the sparkpowder."

"The slave could've been lying. How do we know—"

Ashlok set his jaw. "I'm going in."

Donalek grabbed his arm. "You can't be serious. If you get near that thing, the infection—"

"Remove your hand, Paraplex. Or that drudge's head will not be the last to roll this day." The look in Ashlok's eyes overruled any familial connections.

"Then send a few of the men," Donalek pleaded. "You're a Primus—"

"I could not ask that of another."

The Paraplex's face reddened. He stalked off to oversee the preparation of the sparkpowder charges.

Ashlok turned to address the small raiding party he'd brought up the hill, a dozen exhausted men. "Harken to me, Sons of Mu! Our war against the old masters of the Earth is at an end. The last of the vitaphages hides in this cave. We have no hope of destroying it at this hour. But I will ensure this cave is its tomb."

The men muttered amongst themselves. Ashlok held up a hand to still them.

"When you hear my signal, blow the sparkpowder."

Several men cried out for him to reconsider. There must be some other way. But no! Ashlok needed to see the thing with his eyes to know it was done.

Ashlok took an allicinate torch to ward off the vitaphage's humours and entered the cave. The torch shone off of the craggy rock walls. He kept his axe close in case more drudges were about, but he heard nothing.

At the back of the cave, he found the vitaphage's coffin. Within, the creature slept in the soil of its lost continent of Paramulea. Despite his hatred, Ashlok felt a kind of awe at being in the presence of something that was the last of its kind.

A low thrum filled the chamber, and the coffin lid shifted.

"It's here," Ashlok called over his shoulder. Seconds later, the sparkpowder exploded, the cave shook, rock sealing off the entrance. A gust extinguished his allicinate torch, but it didn't matter. His life might be forfeit. He was not the vitaphage's victim but its pallbearer. Primus Ashlok would carry the last of the old gods to its final resting place in the underworld so the Sons of Mu might live in the light forever and ever.

39 CHILDREN
Matthew Medney

Year: 2566. My name? William Graves, my mission? To figure out how the hell we got here. Where is here, you might ask? Hell. That's here. They came, they saw our technology, and they conquered. That was 150 years ago. The Falic, as they call themselves, are from a star system some 321 light-years away. But all of that is history. We aren't humanity's last hope. We are its reminisce. A last group of survivors of a fallen species used to advance others' hopes and dreams. As I write this, I realize there is no one to read it, but I hope this final mission and one last attempt to save us works. If it doesn't, then it's a pretty bleak story of hubris and failure we wrote for ourselves.

See, we built a vortex. existence. nuclear. occult. machine, or V.E.N.O.M a time dilation inverter. In theory, we should arrive back in 2273, 100 years before they arrived, enough time to solidify our forces and prepare for the impending invasion. But, I must warn you, this is where the story goes from hopeful to suicidal. We will nuke everything within a 10-mile radius of the V.E.N.O.M. It's the only way to bring enough power to the machine. So we'll either arrive back some 300 years or eviscerate the remaining humans and some of these monsters on this planet. If you find this, you'll think we're sadistic, but it's our only hope. Be it a fool's hope.

But if you read this, then you are either in a better future than mine, or you're one of the lonely survivors of this hell on earth.

William, F. Graves.
Scientist. Father. Human.

William signs the notebook, places it gently in the corner of the science lab's remaining desk, and moves towards the door, fondly looking back before carefully closing it and swiftly returning to the test site. The air was barely breathable, and the food was non-existent, he thought to himself as he transversed the waterway, "it would be kinder to just kill everyone." But William was a humanist. He could never fathom an act of that nature, no matter how humanitarian it may be.

So time proceeded as time does, and no more than 17 hours after he finished dotting the i's in his name and leaving the journal for another's eyes, the V.E.N.O.M was ready to change the outcome, through the past or eliminating a future.

The capsule was fitted for 17 males, 28 females, and 39 children. More than 70% of the remaining human population was not in captivity. As they prepared to detonate the bombs and activate the V.E.N.O.M, William thought to himself for one final time. *"At least we went out with a bang."*

Then silence. A silence that was more deafening than any sound could make. Centuries felt to have flashed before William's eyes as he knew he was not dead but could not believe he was alive either. Then, suddenly, it all stopped, and he, like the others, slowly moved to exit the capsule.

It was almost instantly clear that this was not 2273, but much, much, MUCH earlier. Animals of nature that all thought were extinct roamed the lands. Monkeys and Chimps could be heard swinging from tree to tree. Yes, everyone survived the journey, and by some measure of astonishment, the V.E.N.O.M did work. It brought them entirely elsewhere. Did they destroy 2566? Or did they simply and accurately use a time machine. That question would never be answered. But when they were, that was a question that could be.

And then it hit William like a sack of rocks hitting the side door of a sedan. This was not a time or place with a calendar or a society. This was the cradle of life, the beginning of it all. In a moment of existential dread, William understood all.

Like all of humanity, he was in a multi-million-year time loop. The questions flooded his mind… How many times had he been here? How many times had humanity fallen to the Falic…did they know?

We didn't evolve from apes. We came back to start humanity as it was ending. But then, the question of questions fell upon William, and in a last moment of thought, he simply said.

"But where did it begin then?" And with that, William Graves, along with every other adult who was having the same realization, collapsed and died of a brain aneurysm.

Leaving just the children, who had no concept of what had just occurred, to grow, populate, and evolve into the species that would create the first and only ***Time Machine.***

DUSK OF THE FORGOTTEN EARTH

BY PAT SMILET

Following the DNA Wars of 2231 A.D., mankind fell into its final dark age. The last survivors lived in isolated pockets in a desolate land where mutant monsters roamed. In one such settlement in the Bryuo steppe, we find a tribe facing a dire winter.

Their chief Samt mused over their latest ordeal—a brutal ogre (with a bizarre eye mounted on its chest) terrorizing his village. He needed to take action and gathered his hunters to seek help from the gods. The villagers drummed, danced, and chanted ceremonial songs until inspiration struck, and a plan was hatched.

They would lure the beast with a trail of ripe fruit to an isolated mountain spur, a natural fortress with steep, unscalable cliffs, where they'd herded prey for the kill before. They knew the creature liked the fruit because it raided their winter stores often during harvest time.

Hidden behind rocks and bushes, the nervous hunters fiddled with their flint weapons as the ogre crawled into their trap—greedily gobbling up the sweet bait. When the moment was right, Samt whistled the command to attack, and the hunters flung their spears and issued a thunderous cry. The startled ogre swung its flabby arms to block the incoming spears—with every hit, the creature yelped loudly.

Samt sailed between the ogre's swings, dodging sweeping arms to sink his flint blade into the ogre's left leg. The beast's roar sprayed a spittle mist, dosing the hunters in slobber; its chest eye blinked rapidly.

The soaked hunters operated like well-oiled machines and thought they had turned the tide until the ground quaked with a foreboding rhythm. Startled by this new threat, the hunters scattered and hid in the bushes.

A towering giantess appeared and picked up the ogre with surprising gentleness—it was her child. She removed the eye from the ogre's chest and placed it in her empty eye socket (to keep tabs on her child and these pests).

After the pair left, a grim reality dawned on the hunters: They were mere playthings for these monsters.

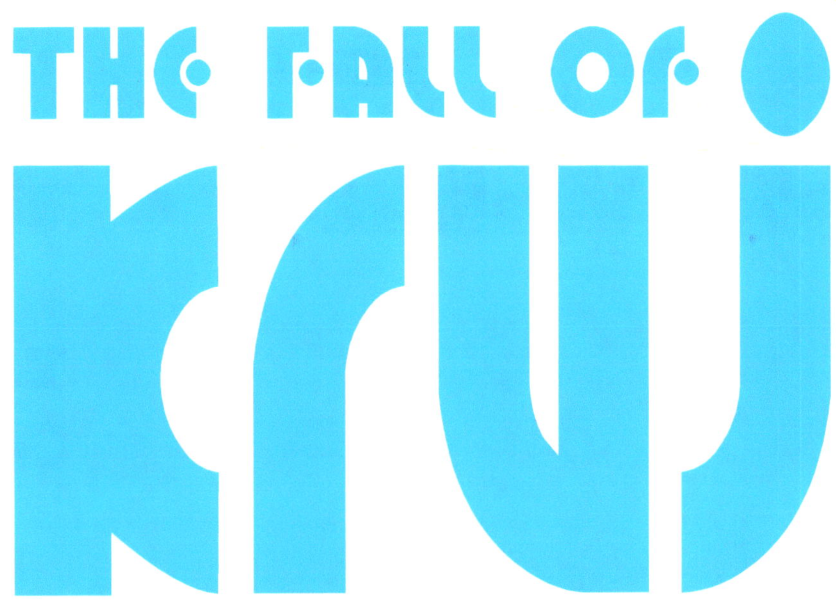

THE FALL OF KRUJ

BY JOHN FROGERT

STREAKS OF LIGHTNING SPARKED AS THE PORTAL GLYPHS slowly faded into the ether. The cheering warriors slammed swords against shields to celebrate as the demons evaporated into banishment. The wizard Garguz faced his army, "We did it!"

They had sacrificed everything to win this bloody war. When Krug materialized with his demon horde, many kingdoms fell quickly under his demonic claw. Only after Garguz mobilized the remaining fragments was he able to rally an army to defeat Kruj.

Ages ago, when the humans fled their world (which succumbed to a magical calamity of their own making), Kruj granted them stay for as long as needed, provided they honored his accords, which they eagerly agreed to follow. The ignorant humans did not know that the blue-skinned demon had transformed a barren dimension into this paradise (fueled by his life-force magic), and their future would be tied to his.

Soon after their arrival, Kruj fell into his required centuries-long slumber to maintain this Eden. Centuries passed, and the humans forgot their debt to Kruj. Library shelves were stuffed with history books that told tales of conquest, of humans overcoming the dangerous lands. The truth about their salvation, about the Kruj's generosity, was lost in the annals of time.

His Wake Day was generally celebrated with weeks of debauchery, not a mustering for banishment. As the glyphs faded, Krug looked upon his fragile masterpiece teetering on the edge of collapse without him, a pretty sick prank on the humans.

Kruj chuckled loudly at the joke as the portal closed. It was the last thing the humans would hear.

THE DOWNFALL OF GREEN STONE

BY ISMAEL GALVAN

WE ALL CHEERED WHEN AGAIL reared her dragon and lifted her sword to the air, declaring that the Orc Army had been defeated at the Battle of Green Stone. We were liberated, free to live in these lands poisoned by dragon bile that seeped into our crops and water. The residue of dragon fire deformed us. Now, we are like creatures in the stories that terrified me as a child.

Early on, before our humanity was erased, we sought help. The cities expected our arrival. They posted signs that declared: People of Green Stone. Keep out! Under threat of death!

"This can't be true," my father said. "They are our friends. We've known them for years. They will receive us."

I was filled with unease and, to this day, regret holding my tongue.

At the city walls, the dragon flag waved. The guard never yelled a warning when he loosed his arrow. My father was hit in the chest. I pulled him away under a hail of arrows. At Green Stone, the people anticipated good news, but their smiles quickly failed when they saw us carrying our friends and crying out for help.

That night, I sat by my father in his room. There wasn't anything we could do besides clean and bandage the wound. In the morning, he was dead.

A year later, we were attacked in the night. Someone yelled, "Fire!" The roofs were stuck with flaming arrows and more alighted the dark sky. I saw men on horseback merrily firing into our village from their direction. We stood among our charred homes in the morning to mourn our dead. The attacks increased along with their cruelty.

We called on villages afflicted by dragon bile to a meeting at Green Stone. Grimwerk from the town of Sword Cliff was a man I respected. After the meetings, we'd sit together.

"I lost my family in the occupation," Grimwerk said. "The orcs killed as though we were excrement on the road. When the dragons came, they were our saviors. Now, we are here."

Grimwerk smoked his pipe. The fire crackled nearby. He continued.

"I had a dream that I was back in the occupation. Though, this time, I was not a man but an orc. The townspeople marched while we whipped them. Then, I saw myself with my family, trying to shield them. So, I drew my dagger and clubbed him to death."

We both paused.

"Dreams reveal secret truths. I deciphered its meaning."

I listened.

"There are no orcs. There never have been. The dragon bile deformed people into monsters like us. This is another iteration."

At the final meeting, Grimwerk proposed a plan to kill their smaller male dragons, leaving Agail's dragon as a lone mother. The leaders agreed to make war.

At the winter solstice festival, we watched from cover until the celebration died in the late hour. We entered the city through the sewer in dark cloaks, passed under shadows, and converged on the dragon stable.

Though a wall protected the stable, its defenses were designed against men. Our weapons were crude, but the dragon bile increased our savagery. We slaughtered the guards with quiet ferocity, blades stabbing arteries that gushed blood as we held them down. We paused at the windows and listened. A few handlers were in the kitchen having a late drink and smoking herb. We fell on them like wolves.

"The stable is ours," Grimwerk said.

Our party breathed heavily as we waited for our hearts to subside. We entered the main stable, a circular structure housing the dragons along the perimeter. But my eyes fell on the center of a grand marble statue of Agail raising her sword atop her dragon, as I remember seeing long ago.

"Varis," Grimwerk called me to refocus.

The dragons were younglings. They eyed us suspiciously but were domesticated enough to remain calm. We tossed meat laced with sleeping herbs into each stall. The effect required time, but they all collapsed.

"Make quick work of them," Grimwerk said. "We cannot risk them with clear minds."

I entered a stall and found a blue dragon lolling on the ground. Even as a youngling, the creature's vicious body filled me with fear. I kneeled by the dragon's head. Its dreamy eye beheld me in confusion. I plunged my dagger into its throat. The dragon struggled weakly and then bled out on the floor.

After murdering the dragons, we met by the statue of Agail. Our bodies were covered in the butchery. Grimwerk decapitated a dragon and stuck the head on Agail's sword. Gore dripped over her. "All hail the dragon queen," he said.

Yes, covered in blood, she was exactly as I remembered her at the Battle of Green Stone.

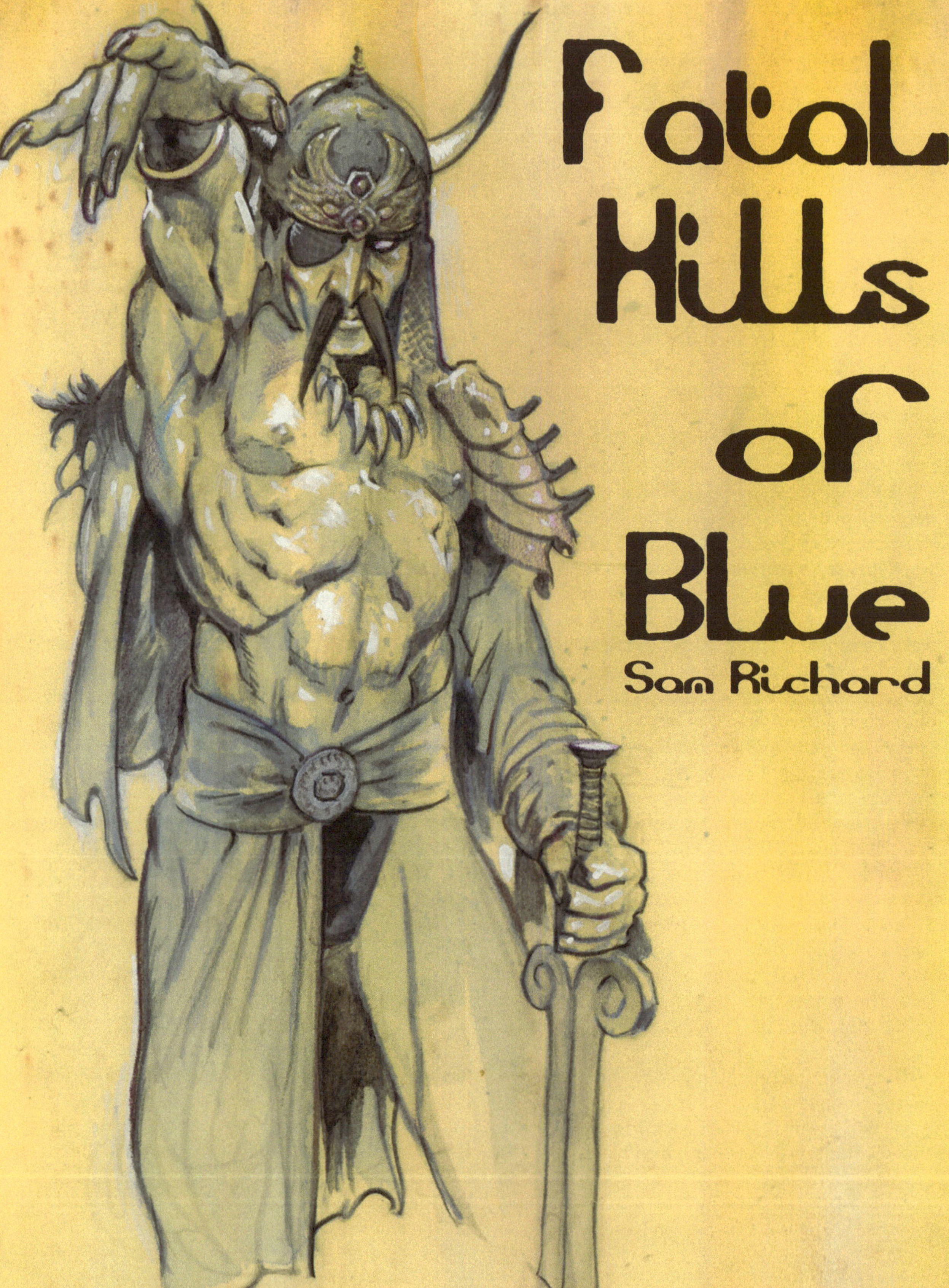
Fatal Hills of Blue
Sam Richard

On the Cerulean Fields where wise men dare not go, Bartak draws his sword and quiets his breath, gripping the rope so tight it cuts into his swollen palm. His silence comes too late. Below him, the ground undulates and twists; patterns scrawled in secret glyphs beneath his feet. The disturbance kicks up pollen and black soil, blanketing the fields in rich azure mist. It tickles his nose and he steadies himself for the coming violence.

The sweet, almost silent moment before the storm of flesh and fang. The clash of iron and bone. Red of tooth and claw. It pulses within him seductively. Impatiently. But all remains quiet, but for the shifting earth.

He tries to drop the rope, but it's bored into his palm, tacky with blood. Blood he can smell, some fresh and delicious. Eventually the rope falls to his feet. It is glorious to unburden himself for a moment; his shoulders cracking from the weighted journey.

One final piece. One final blessing. One final curse.

He spits blue grit from his mouth and walks silently through the lush hills, sweat crawling behind his patch and stinging the fresh wound in his eye – a gift from a friend. So strange to be surrounded by such growth; such ancient, terrifying, and beautiful growth. Unlike the world beyond. Nothing but gray stone and black sands; desperate people huddled together in makeshift cities, living their tiny lives. Afraid.

Cowards.

Removing his helm, he mops sweat from his brow, looking off into the unending sea of blue. The barely-alive thing attached to the rope moans. Its ganglionic flesh shimmers like hardened leather in the sun. A hint of dulled cobalt suddenly glowing under the surface of its skin.

The earth shakes and crests with renewed violence, jagged stone pillars breaking through the soil. And yet the flowers remain peaceful, swaying gently in the breeze. The quake pulls him to the ground. Before he can right himself the beast he'd been dragging rises. Right on cue.

It rushes him, glint of steel in its pale yellow eyes. Gnarled limbs drag behind the beast as it runs, collecting jagged pieces of shattered stone in its bizarrely glowing flesh. It's fast. Too fast to strike before it bridges the gap, swinging its arms wildly, clashing against his sword. Shoving Bartak back, teetering at the edge of a crater left by one of the stone pillars.

Locked in embrace, Bartak drags his blade across the ridged edges of the beast's arms. It wasn't this strong when he defeated it before. But it also wasn't breathing in the carbon remains of its ancestors. He pushes the blade down then back up before the gnarled thing has a change to react. His steel cleaves through its torso, opening its stomach like a cave.

Foul orange pustules splatter at both their feet.

One final piece. One final blessing. One final curse.

Bartak grabs one of the shimmering boils from the dirt. Crusted with blue pollen and dark grit, he doesn't hesitate to throw it into his mouth, piercing it with his teeth. Malodorous fluid fills his throat.

Below, the quake returns. Up from the fissures surrounding the pillars, rises a gangle of sleek, sharpened claws all moving as one. They rupture the earth as they squeeze in on the warrior, tearing through the rock like tender flesh.

He swings his sword, metal clanging off of the hardened shell of this new threat. But there are too many of them, all slicing and tearing at him. All surrounding him. And then the ground disappears beneath, as he is pulled under into the darkness.

There is no moment for the dust to settle. He is encased in the clawed hand of a giant ghastly fox-like creature. It towers over him, it's sallow matted flesh both rotting and in the midst of dry decay. The claw tightens, as the monster stares at him, contemplating something he'll never understand. It's beyond time. It's why he's here.

Without warning or sound, it tosses Bartak into its open mouth. He lands on the tongue with a wet slap. Surrounded by row after row of jagged, rotting teeth, he propels himself towards the throat. The tongue shifts, trying to maintain control, trying to smash him beneath its mandible, but he's too fast, sliding down the gullet and into the open throat of the beast.

Beyond feculent, beyond darkness, Bartak bursts through the windpipe, sword first, into the atrium, which beats greedily. The beast shrieks above.

Gritting his teeth, Bartak pierces through the inner membrane of the polyp and spits the juices all over the heart of the beast. It jumps and hisses as the muscle begins to dissolve.

For Bartak, this is only the beginning:

One final piece.
One final blessing.
One final curse.

STONE SKIN
by Cody Goodfellow

When **she could run** no further into the swamp, when the most dogged of her pursuers had given up the chase, she looked about her and saw the other-men, the circling lizards and gliding pythons drawing closer on all sides.

Driven from her nest of pelts beside a dying fire by the ones who'd ambushed her mate as he limped wounded back from the hunt. His usurpers spurned her and drove her into the swamp with rocks and blows when they found she was heavy with Long-Arm's children. Twins, the old women said—an ill omen that had now come to pass.

With nowhere else to go, she had thought to return to her own clan in the next valley, a small band of gatherers from whom she was taken in a raid when she was little more than a girl. But Long-Arm's rivals had pelted her with stones and herded her into the swamp, and no sooner had she lost them she was hopelessly lost herself.

She wallowed into a clearing in the mangrove trees, black water sparkling under the wide yellow eye of the moon. Before her, a monolithic tower of strange black stone loomed up to rake the black sky, itself split and crowned by a huge, thrusting tree. Brutish grunts and hoots echoed through the swamp as the bestial other-men warily skulked down from the trees and out into the open, braving the predators to get at her.

The brackish water rose up to her shaking legs, burning hips, and gravid belly. An undulating coil of muscle looped around her leg, dragging her down into the bottomless muck as the fanged maw unhinged its jaw to swallow her whole.

A lambent-eyed lizard snapped at the serpent's head, and they thrashed about her. The beast men cowered, waiting for their share of the battle's carnage. There was no hope, none to cry for. The headless python's death throes pulled her down into the sucking mud, but she cried out, and just before her face was drawn beneath the waters, she heard an answer.

How fitting that this one, too, had come to claim a piece of her.

They called him Stone-Skin. Cursed with a misshapen foot and an ill-formed eye, he was used as bait to trap in the hunt but somehow always came back while his cruel peers returned mauled or not at all. Banished to the swamp, he thrived and became a sort of totem to the tribe that cast him out. All that went ill with the hunt or the watering hole or the weather, Stone-Skin was behind it. Yet when the hot-headed young men endured their first hunt alone in the swamp and sought to make good on boasts, they would take the outcast's head once and for all. None caught so much as a glimpse of the lurking scourge, and many supposed him long dead.

Now she saw but dimly his knurled form crouched atop the sundered boulder, clutching the shaft of a sharpened branch as if poised to hurl it at her attackers or at her. Mud encrusted his flesh, and moss and stranger growths grew on him so that only a stray beam of moonlight through the ragged clouds set him apart from the rugose bark of the tree trunk at his back.

None of the other-men seemed to see him. He could afford to watch the outcome and pick off the weakest. He had become something stranger than the other-men who never left the trees, so eating her flesh, to such a thing, would be no taboo.

But he barked a reply to her wordless cry for help, a strange cry because the voice was so unused to the crude tongue of her people.

"Smoke-hair!"

Her head whipped round amid churning foam, her view obscured by wild black hair whipping across her face, and she knew the strange cry named her, as not even her parents, long dead and gone, nor her mate had ever thought to name her.

At the moment of her death, from the lips of this brutish freak, she had a name.

The noisome waters closed over her head. Forced itself into her mouth and nostrils. As her last bubbles of breath escaped her, she clawed at slimy scales and spasming muscle, kicked at rotten deadfalls and sucking mud, and made peace with her end.

Suddenly, the bands of constricting muscle around her leg went limp. Struggling, she broke the surface and gasped a burning breath. The great crocodile lurched backward with the python still clasped in its jaws, the sharpened wooden shaft transfixing its skull, then floated away like a deadfall log.

She found her footing and shrugged off the twitching coils of serpent flesh just as the other-men drew near. Their instinctual fear of the open ground gave way to hunger and lust, and their grunts and hoots turned to warlike cries and growls at each other and at the interloper watching from atop the crown of boulders.

Crooked plunged a broken branch into a fissure in the towering boulder and throttled it, kicking at the stones, seeming to rage impotently at the bestial troop, but did nothing more to save her.

She staggered, hopeless and undone by fatigue, yet flashing broken nails and baring her teeth at the other-men, but her threat displays only whetted their appetite. Closer still they stalked, the largest and most savage of them clouting the others aside as he advanced to claim his prize.

All her life, she had been fought over, protected by, abused, and used by men. None had shown her a moment's tenderness, and she had known nothing more pleasurable than their absence until Long-Arm gave her children. The strange sensation deep inside her quickened an impulse she had never felt before in all her short, brutish life—it was a promise of something, new of the undoing of her dreary existence, and she felt buoyed by a new determination to fight for them, as she never had, for herself.

Smoke-Hair would make him pay dearly for it.

Defiantly, she raked the murky water and waded backward, daring the beast to follow her, to go deeper. His scarred features knit in a ferocious snarl, and he beat his shaggy breast, but she saw the primal fear behind it. He looked back to his troop, stomping and roaring in the shallows, just as Stone-Skin again called her name.

"Smoke-Hair!"

She looked up and reeled with the impossibility of the sight that met her eyes. The enormous boulder at which Stone-Skin had been working with the branch suddenly fell away from the rocky tower and crushed half the other-men into the mud.

The splash from the boulder knocked the other-man chieftain facedown in the mud. Smoke-Hair stumbled and fell, paddling and kicking away from the struggling beast, but a taloned paw seized her ankle and dragged her backward.

She fought as she was pulled under the mud again, but the other-man's hold could not be broken. Unable to swim in water above his waist, the ape clung to her and twisted her leg so she could not find the surface.

Through a stream of escaping breath, she saw the distorted image of Stone-Skin diving into the water. The grip on her ankle spasmed and withdrew. Smoke-Hair kicked for the surface and turned to see Stone-Skin and the other-man tossing and thrashing beneath the churning water. Grappling in the dark water, they disappeared beneath a red miasma that slowly subsided until the pool's surface was deathly still.

The surviving other-men gibbered and howled, but none approached her or the grisly site of their chief's demise. And Stone-Skin…?

All at once, the brute lurched upright, still cradling the drowned other-man with an iron arm around his crushed throat. He'd endured a grievous mauling, but his lungs held enough breath to bellow a challenge that sent the decimated troop scurrying back to the trees.

Now, they stood almost close enough to touch, and Smoke-Hair dared to look her savior in his evil eye. In that crooked, battered face, she saw something she had never beheld or hoped to find in the face of another.

In that face, she saw one who did not see her as prey or property. His hand thrust out not to take her by the hair or the throat but gently stroked the swelling of her belly, and a peculiar expression stole across his brutish, crooked features. Teeth bared, but not in aggression; eyes downcast but lambent with a strange inner light. "Smoke-Hair," he murmured, letting his hand fall away from her as if she might burn him.

And then she looked behind him as a groaning became a deafening roar, and the gigantic tree that had split the rocky tower faltered and tumbled down on top of them.

Thicker than a tall man's height, the massive trunk would have crushed them into the mud, but Stone-Skin threw out his arms and caught it. He strained to hold up the crushing weight as he sank into the mud.

Stumbling, she clung to Stone-Skin, felt his chest heaving with impossible effort, his thews throbbing, joints popping, but he refused to buckle. The unbearable weight drove him deeper into the water, but somehow, he took the trunk across his shoulders to free an arm to push her away.

She resisted, but now he growled threateningly and shoved her out from under the trembling fallen tree just as its bulk drove him down until the water lapped at his chin. She fell backward and kicked at the mud, looking back at him and crying out his name.

Her last glimpse of her savior was of those knurled arms and grasping paws, battling to the last against the tree trunk that had augured him into the mud before the trunk sank into the pool where he'd stood with a sickening splash.

Silence reigned briefly before the swamp's nocturnal denizens resumed their mating and death-cries. Smoke-Hair shakily staggered out of the pool against a feeble current of fresher water, heading towards the stream and, she hoped, the territory of her birth-clan. What would she tell them? What would she tell her unborn children when they ask about their father?

She would tell them nothing of Long-Arm and his treacherous clan, but she would tell her tribe about the outcast who used wit and brawn and even his life to deliver her from the predators of the swamp and who gave her a name…and whose name would live on as long as tales were told over fires, as protection against the darkness.

As she began to climb up the winding valley beside a clear mountain stream, she almost thought she heard her name once more, echoing through the fetid maze of the swamp at her back, but when she turned, she saw only the wall of trees, gray in the moonlight, like cliffs of stone skin.

FORBIDDEN FUTURES

THE SHADOW KINGDOM
by Robert E. Howard

I. A KING COMES RIDING

The blare of the trumpets grew louder, like a deep golden tide surge, like the soft booming of the evening tides against the silver beaches of Valusia. The throng shouted, women flung roses from the roofs as the rhythmic chiming of silver hoofs came clearer and the first of the mighty array swung into view in the broad white street that curved round the golden-spired Tower of Splendor.

First came the trumpeters, slim youths, clad in scarlet, riding with a flourish of long, slender golden trumpets; next the bowmen, tall men from the mountains; and behind these the heavily armed footmen, their broad shields clashing in unison, their long spears swaying in perfect rhythm to their stride. Behind them came the mightiest soldiery in all the world, the Red Slayers, horsemen, splendidly mounted, armed in red from helmet to spur. Proudly they sat their steeds, looking neither to right nor to left, but aware of the shouting for all that. Like bronze statues they were, and there was never a waver in the forest of spears that reared above them.

Behind those proud and terrible ranks came the motley files of the mercenaries, fierce, wild-looking warriors, men of Mu and of Kaa-u and of the hills of the east and the isles of the west. They bore spears and heavy swords, and a compact group that marched somewhat apart were the bowmen of Lemuria. Then came the light foot of the nation, and more trumpeters brought up the rear.

A brave sight, and a sight which aroused a fierce thrill in the soul of Kull, king of Valusia. Not on the Topaz Throne at the front of the regal Tower of Splendor sat Kull, but in the saddle, mounted on a great stallion, a true warrior king. His mighty arm swung up in reply to the salutes as the hosts passed. His fierce eyes passed the gorgeous trumpeters with a casual glance, rested longer on the following soldiery; they blazed with a ferocious light as the Red Slayers halted in front of him with a clang of arms and a rearing of steeds, and tendered him the crown salute. They narrowed slightly as the mercenaries strode by. They saluted no one, the mercenaries. They walked with shoulders flung back, eyeing Kull boldly and straightly, albeit with a certain appreciation; fierce eyes, unblinking; savage eyes, staring from beneath shaggy manes and heavy brows.

And Kull gave back a like stare. He granted much to brave men, and there were no braver in all the world, not even among the wild tribesmen who now disowned him. But Kull was too much the savage to have any great love for these. There were too many feuds. Many were age-old enemies of Kull's nation, and though the name of Kull was now a word accursed among the mountains and valleys of his people, and though Kull had put them from his mind, yet the old hates, the ancient passions still lingered. For Kull was no Valusian but an Atlantean.

The armies swung out of sight around the gem-blazing shoulders of the Tower of Splendor and Kull reined his stallion about and started toward the palace at an easy gait, discussing the review with the commanders that rode with him, using not many words, but saying much.

"The army is like a sword," said Kull, "and must not be allowed to rust." So down the street they rode, and Kull gave no heed to any of the whispers that reached his hearing from the throngs that still swarmed the streets.

"That is Kull, see! Valka! But what a king! And what a man! Look at his arms! His shoulders!"

And an undertone of more sinister whisperings: "Kull! Ha, accursed usurper from the pagan isles"— "Aye, shame to Valusia that a barbarian sits on the Throne of Kings."

Little did Kull heed. Heavy-handed had he seized the decaying throne of ancient Valusia and with a heavier hand did he hold it, a man against a nation.

After the council chamber, the social palace where Kull replied to the formal and laudatory phrases of the lords and ladies, with carefully hidden, grim amusement at such frivolities; then the lords and ladies took their formal departure and Kull leaned back upon the ermine throne and contemplated matters of state until an attendant requested permission from the great king to speak, and announced an emissary from the Pictish embassy.

Kull brought his mind back from the dim mazes of Valusian statecraft where it had been wandering, and gazed upon the Pict with little favor. The man gave back the gaze of the king without flinching. He was a lean-hipped, massive-chested warrior of middle height, dark, like all his race, and strongly built. From strong, immobile features gazed dauntless and inscrutable eyes.

"The chief of the Councilors, Ka-nu of the tribe, right hand of the king of Pictdom, sends greetings and says: 'There is a throne at the feast of the rising moon for Kull, king of kings, lord of lords, emperor of Valusia.'"

"Good," answered Kull. "Say to Ka-nu the Ancient, ambassador of the western isles, that the king of Valusia will quaff wine with him when the moon floats over the hills of Zalgara."

Still the Pict lingered. "I have a word for the king, not"—with a contemptuous flirt of his hand—"for these slaves."

Kull dismissed the attendants with a word, watching the Pict warily.

The man stepped nearer, and lowered his voice; "Come alone to feast tonight, lord king. Such was the word of my chief."

The king's eyes narrowed, gleam-ing like gray sword steel, coldly.

"Alone?"

"Aye."

They eyed each other silently, their mutual tribal enmity seething beneath their cloak of formality. Their mouths spoke the cultured speech, the conventional court phrases of a highly polished race, a race not their own, but from their eyes gleamed the primal traditions of the elemental savage. Kull might be the king of Valusia and the Pict might be an emissary to her courts, but there in the throne hall of kings, two tribesmen glowered at each other, fierce and wary, while ghosts of wild wars and world-ancient feuds whispered to each.

To the king was the advantage and he enjoyed it to its fullest extent. Jaw resting on hand, he eyed the Pict, who stood like an image of bronze, head flung back, eyes unflinching.

Across Kull's lips stole a smile that was more a sneer.

"And so I am to come—alone?" Civilization had taught him to speak by innuendo and the Pict's dark eyes glittered, though he made no reply. "How am I to know that you come from Ka-nu?"

"I have spoken," was the sullen response.

"And when did a Pict speak truth?" sneered Kull, fully aware that the Picts never lied, but using this means to enrage the man.

"I see your plan, king," the Pict answered imperturbably. "You wish to anger me. By Valka, you need go no further! I am angry enough. And I challenge you to meet me in single battle, spear, sword or dagger, mounted or afoot. Are you king or man?"

Kull's eyes glinted with the grudging admiration a warrior must needs give a bold foeman, but he did not fail to use the chance of further annoying his antagonist.

"A king does not accept the challenge of a nameless savage," he sneered, "nor does the emperor of Valusia break the Truce of Ambassadors. You have leave to go. Say to Ka-nu I will come alone."

The Pict's eyes flashed murderously. He fairly shook in the grasp of the primitive blood-lust; then, turning his back squarely upon the king of Valusia, he strode across the Hall of Society and vanished through the great door.

Again Kull leaned back upon the ermine throne and meditated.

So the chief of the Council of Picts wished him to come alone? But for what reason? Treachery? Grimly Kull touched the hilt of his great sword. But scarcely. The Picts valued too greatly the alliance with Valusia to break it for any feudal reason. Kull might be a warrior of Atlantis and hereditary enemy of all Picts, but too, he was king of Valusia, the most potent ally of the Men of the West.

Kull reflected long upon the strange state of affairs that made him ally of ancient foes and foe of ancient friends. He rose and paced restlessly across the hall, with the quick, noiseless tread of a lion. Chains of friendship, tribe and tradition had he broken to satisfy his ambition. And, by Valka, god of the sea and the land, he had realized that ambition! He was king of Valusia—a fading, degenerate Valusia, a Valusia living mostly in dreams of bygone glory, but still a mighty land and the greatest of the Seven Empires. Valusia—Land of Dreams, the tribesmen named it, and sometimes it seemed to Kull that he moved in a dream. Strange to him were the intrigues of court and palace, army and people. All was like a masquerade, where men and women hid their real thoughts with a smooth mask. Yet the seizing of the throne had been easy—a bold snatching of opportunity, the swift whirl of swords, the slaying of a tyrant of whom men had wearied unto death, short, crafty plotting with ambitious statesmen out of favor at court—and Kull, wandering adventurer, Atlantean exile, had swept up to the dizzy heights of his dreams: he was lord of Valusia, king of kings. Yet now it seemed that the seizing was far easier than the keeping. The sight of the Pict had brought back youthful associations to his mind, the free, wild savagery of his boyhood. And now a strange feeling of dim unrest, of unreality, stole over him as of late it had been doing. Who was he, a straightforward man of the seas and the mountain, to rule a race strangely and terribly wise with the mysticisms of antiquity? An ancient race—

"I am Kull!" said he, flinging back his head as a lion flings back his mane. "I am Kull!"

His falcon gaze swept the ancient hall. His self-confidence flowed back. . . . And in a dim nook of the hall a tapestry moved—slightly.

2. THUS SPAKE THE SILENT HALLS OF VALUSIA

The moon had not risen, and the garden was lighted with torches aglow in silver cressets when Kull sat down in the throne before the table of Ka-nu, ambassador of the western isles. At his right hand sat the ancient Pict, as much unlike an emissary of that fierce race as a man could be. Ancient was Ka-nu and wise in statecraft, grown old in the game. There was no elemental hatred in the eyes that looked at Kull appraisingly; no tribal traditions hindered his judgments. Long associations with the statesmen of the civilized nations had swept away such cobwebs. Not: who and what is this man? was the question ever foremost in Ka-nu's mind, but: can I use this man, and how? Tribal prejudices he used only to further his own schemes.

And Kull watched Ka-nu, answering his conversation briefly, wondering if civilization would make of him a thing like the Pict. For Ka-nu was soft and paunchy. Many years had stridden across the sky-rim since Ka-nu had wielded a sword. True, he was old, but Kull had seen men older than he in the forefront of battle. The Picts were a long-lived race. A beautiful girl stood at Ka-nu's elbow, refilling his goblet, and she was kept busy. Meanwhile Ka-nu kept up a running fire of jests and comments, and Kull, secretly contemptuous of his garrulity, nevertheless missed none of his shrewd humor.

At the banquet were Pictish chiefs and statesmen, the latter jovial and easy in their manner, the warriors formally courteous, but plainly hampered by their tribal affinities. Yet Kull, with a tinge of envy, was cognizant of the freedom and ease of the affair as contrasted with like affairs of the Valusian court. Such freedom prevailed in the rude camps of Atlantis—Kull shrugged his shoulders. After all, doubtless Ka-nu, who had seemed to have forgotten he was a Pict as far as time-hoary custom and prejudice went, was right and he, Kull, would better become a Valusian in mind as in name.

At last when the moon had reached her zenith, Ka-nu, having eaten and drunk as much as any three men there, leaned back upon his divan with a comfortable sigh and said, "Now, get you gone, friends, for the king and I would converse on such matters as concerns not children. Yes, you too, my pretty; yet first let me kiss those ruby lips—so; now dance away, my rose-bloom."

Ka-nu's eyes twinkled above his white beard as he surveyed Kull, who sat erect, grim and uncompromising.

"You are thinking, Kull," said the old statesman, suddenly, "that Ka-nu is a useless old reprobate, fit for nothing except to guzzle wine and kiss wenches!"

In fact, this remark was so much in line with his actual thoughts, and so plainly put, that Kull was rather startled, though he gave no sign.

Ka-nu gurgled and his paunch shook with his mirth. "Wine is red and women are soft," he remarked tolerantly. "But—ha! ha!—think not old Ka-nu allows either to interfere with business."

Again he laughed, and Kull moved restlessly. This seemed much like being made sport of, and the king's scintillant eyes began to glow with a feline light.

Ka-nu reached for the wine-pitcher, filled his beaker and glanced questioningly at Kull, who shook his head irritably.

"Aye," said Ka-nu equably, "it takes an old head to stand strong drink. I am growing old, Kull, so why should you young men begrudge me such pleasures as we oldsters must find? Ah me, I grow ancient and withered, friendless and cheerless."

But his looks and expressions failed far of bearing out his words. His rubicund countenance fairly glowed, and his eyes sparkled, so that his white beard seemed incongruous. Indeed, he looked remarkably elfin, reflected Kull, who felt vaguely resentful. The old scoundrel had lost all of the primitive virtues of his race and of Kull's race, yet he seemed more pleased in his aged days than otherwise.

"Hark ye, Kull," said Ka-nu, raising an admonitory finger, "'tis a chancy thing to laud a young man, yet I must speak my true thoughts to gain your confidence."

"If you think to gain it by flattery—"

"Tush. Who spake of flattery? I flatter only to disguard."

There was a keen sparkle in Ka-nu's eyes, a cold glimmer that did not match his lazy smile. He knew men, and he knew that to gain his end he must smite straight with this tigerish barbarian, who, like a wolf scenting a snare, would scent out unerringly any falseness in the skein of his word-web.

"You have power, Kull," said he, choosing his words with more care than he did in the council rooms of the nation, "to make yourself mightiest of all kings, and restore some of the lost glories of Valusia. So. I care little for Valusia—though the women and wine be excellent—save for the fact that the stronger Valusia is, the stronger is the Pict nation. More, with an Atlantean on the throne, eventually Atlantis will become united—"

Kull laughed in harsh mockery. Ka-nu had touched an old wound.

"Atlantis made my name accursed when I went to seek fame and fortune among the cities of the world. We—they—are age-old foes of the Seven Empires, are age-old foes of the allies of the Empires, as you should know."

Ka-nu tugged his beard and smiled enigmatically.

"Nay, nay. Let it pass. But I know whereof I speak. And then warfare will cease, wherein there is no gain; I see a world of peace and prosperity—man loving his fellow man—the good supreme. All this can you accomplish—if you live!"

"Ha!" Kull's lean hand closed on his hilt and he half rose, with a sudden movement of such dynamic speed that Ka-nu, who fancied men as some men fancy blooded horses, felt his old blood leap with a sudden thrill. Valka, what a warrior! Nerves and sinews of steel and fire, bound together with the perfect co-ordination, the fighting instinct, that makes the terrible warrior.

But none of Ka-nu's enthusiasm showed in his mildly sarcastic tone.

"Tush. Be seated. Look about you. The gardens are deserted, the seats empty, save for ourselves. You fear not me?"

Kull sank back, gazing about him warily.

"There speaks the savage," mused Ka-nu. "Think you if I planned treachery I would enact it here where suspicion would be sure to fall upon me? Tut.

You young tribesmen have much to learn. There were my chiefs who were not at ease because you were born among the hills of Atlantis, and you despise me in your secret mind because I am a Pict. Tush. I see you as Kull, king of Valusia, not as Kull, the reckless Atlantean, leader of the raiders who harried the western isles. So you should see in me, not a Pict but an international man, a figure of the world. Now to that figure, hark! If you were slain tomorrow who would be king?"

"Kaanuub, baron of Blaal."

"Even so. I object to Kaanuub for many reasons, yet most of all for the fact that he is but a figurehead."

"How so? He was my greatest opponent, but I did not know that he championed any cause but his own."

"The night can hear," answered Ka-nu obliquely. "There are worlds within worlds. But you may trust me and you may trust Brule, the Spear-slayer. Look!" He drew from his robes a bracelet of gold representing a winged dragon coiled thrice, with three horns of ruby on the head.

"Examine it closely. Brule will wear it on his arm when he comes to you tomorrow night so that you may know him. Trust Brule as you trust yourself, and do what he tells you to. And in proof of trust, look ye!"

And with the speed of a striking hawk, the ancient snatched something from his robes, something that flung a weird green light over them, and which he replaced in an instant.

"The stolen gem!" exclaimed Kull, recoiling. "The green jewel from the Temple of the Serpent! Valka! You! And why do you show it to me?"

"To save your life. To prove my trust. If I betray your trust, deal with me likewise. You hold my life in your hand. Now I could not be false to you if I would, for a word from you would be my, doom."

Yet for all his words the old scoundrel beamed merrily and seemed vastly pleased with himself.

"But why do you give me this hold over you?" asked Kull, becoming more bewildered each second.

"As I told you. Now, you see that I do not intend to deal you false, and tomorrow night when Brule comes to you, you will follow his advice without fear of treachery. Enough. An escort waits outside to ride to the palace with you, lord."

Kull rose. "But you have told me nothing."

"Tush. How impatient are youths!" Ka-nu looked more like a mischievous elf than ever. "Go you and dream of thrones and power and kingdoms, while I dream of wine and soft women and roses. And fortune ride with you, King Kull."

As he left the garden, Kull glanced back to see Ka-nu still reclining lazily in his seat, a merry ancient, beaming on all the world with jovial fellowship.

A mounted warrior waited for the king just without the garden and Kull was slightly surprised to see that it was the same that had brought Ka-nu's invitation. No word was spoken as Kull swung into the saddle nor as they clattered along the empty streets.

The color and the gayety of the day had given away to the eery stillness of night. The city's antiquity was more than ever apparent beneath the bent, silver moon. The huge pillars of the mansions and palaces towered up into the stars. The broad stairways, silent and deserted, seemed to climb endlessly until they vanished in the shadowy darkness of the upper realms. Stairs to the stars, thought Kull, his imaginative mind inspired by the weird grandeur of the scene.

Clang! clang! clang! sounded the silver hoofs on the broad, moon-flooded streets, but otherwise there was no sound. The age of the city, its incredible antiquity, was almost oppressive to the king; it was as if the great silent buildings laughed at him, noiselessly, with unguessable mockery. And what secrets did they hold?

"You are young," said the palaces and the temples and the shrines, "but we are old. The world was wild with youth when we were reared. You and your tribe shall pass, but we are invincible, indestructible. We towered above a strange world, ere Atlantis and Lemuria rose from the sea; we still shall reign when the green waters sigh for many a restless fathom above the spires of Lemuria and the hills of Atlantis and when the isles of the Western Men are the mountains of a strange land."

"How many kings have we watched ride down these streets before Kull of Atlantis was even a dream in the mind of Ka, bird of Creation? Ride on, Kull of Atlantis; greater shall follow you; greater came before you. They are dust; they are forgotten; we stand; we know; we are. Ride, ride on, Kull of Atlantis; Kull the king, Kull the fool!"

And it seemed to Kull that the clashing hoofs took up the silent refrain to beat it into the night with hollow re-echoing mockery:

"Kull—the—king! Kull—the—fool!"

Glow, moon; you light a king's way! Gleam, stars; you are torches in the train of an emperor! And clang, silver-shod hoofs; you herald that Kull rides through Valusia.

Ho! Awake, Valusia! It is Kull that rides, Kull the king!

"We have known many kings," said the silent halls of Valusia.

And so in a brooding mood Kull came to the palace, where his bodyguard, men of the Red Slayers, came to take the rein of the great stallion and escort Kull to his rest. There the Pict, still sullenly speechless, wheeled his steed with a savage wrench of the rein and fled away in the dark like a phantom; Kull's heightened imagination pictured him speeding through the silent streets like a goblin out of the Elder World.

There was no sleep for Kull that night, for it was nearly dawn and he spent the rest of the night hours pacing the throneroom, and pondering over what had passed. Ka-nu had told him nothing, yet he had put himself in Kull's complete power. At what had he hinted when he had said the baron of Blaal was naught but a figurehead? And who was this Brule who was to come to him by night, wearing the mystic armlet of the dragon? And why? Above all, why had Ka-nu shown him the green gem of terror, stolen long ago from the temple of the Serpent, for which the world would rock in wars were it known to the weird and terrible keepers of that temple, and from whose vengeance not even Ka-nu's ferocious tribesmen might be able to save him? But Ka-nu knew he was safe, reflected Kull, for the statesman was too shrewd to expose himself to risk without profit. But was it to throw the king off his guard and pave the way to treachery? Would Ka-nu dare let him live now? Kull shrugged his shoulders.

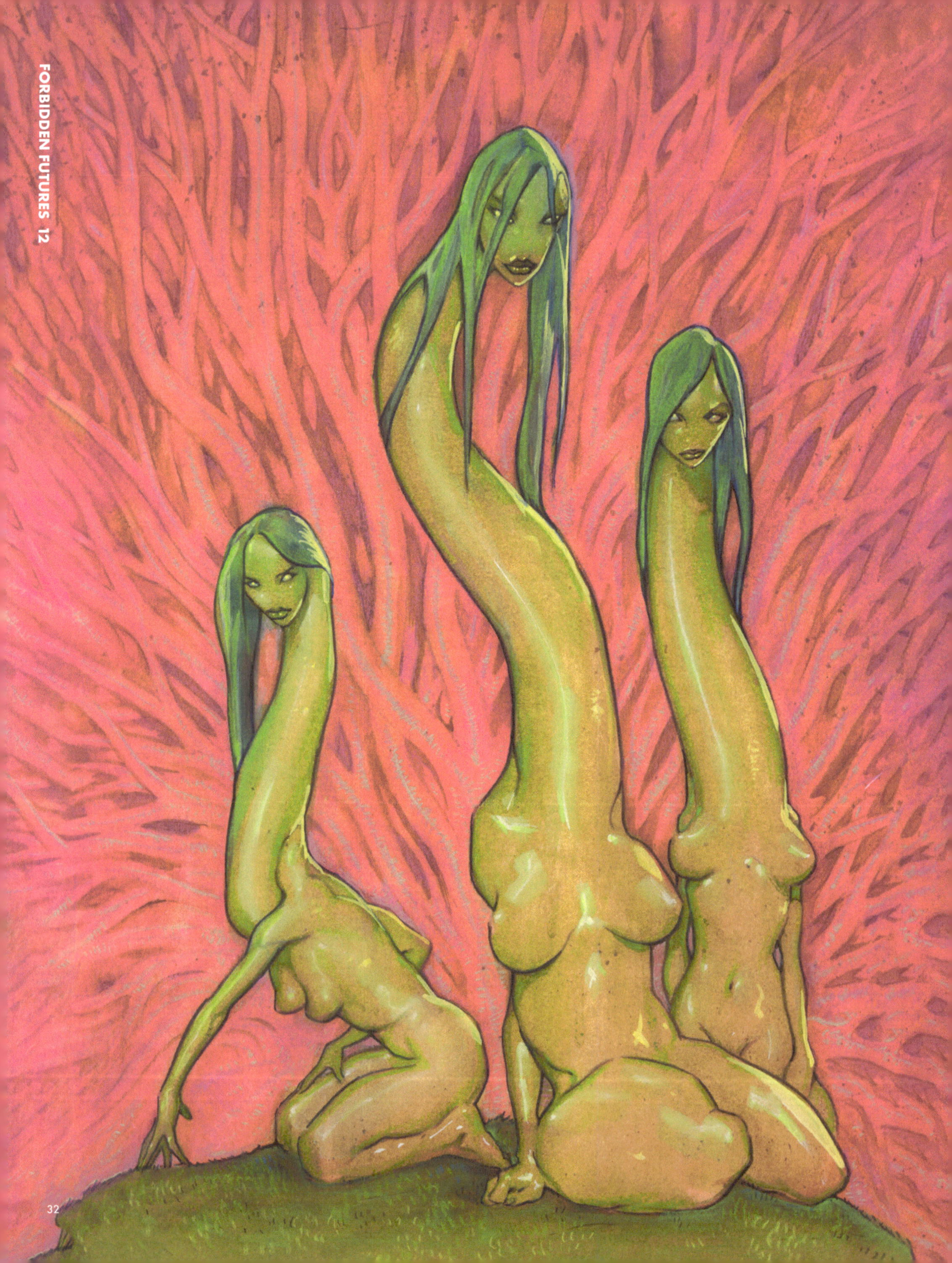

3. THEY THAT WALK THE NIGHT

The moon had not risen when Kull, hand to hilt, stepped to a window. The windows opened upon the great inner gardens of the royal palace, and the breezes of the night, bearing the scents of spice trees, blew the filmy curtains about. The king looked out. The walks and groves were deserted; carefully trimmed trees were bulky shadows; fountains near by flung their slender sheen of silver in the starlight and distant fountains rippled steadily. No guards walked those gardens, for so closely were the outer walls guarded that it seemed impossible for any invader to gain access to them.

Vines curled up the walls of the palace, and even as Kull mused upon the ease with which they might be climbed, a segment of shadow detached itself from the darkness below the window and a bare, brown arm curved up over the sill. Kull's great sword hissed half-way from the sheath; then the king halted. Upon the muscular forearm gleamed the dragon armlet shown him by Ka-nu the night before.

The possessor of the arm pulled himself up over the sill and into the room with the swift, easy motion of a climbing leopard.

"You are Brule?" asked Kull, and then stopped in surprize not unmingled with annoyance and suspicion; for the man was he whom Kull had taunted in the hall of Society; the same who had escorted him from the Pictish embassy.

"I am Brule, the Spear-slayer," answered the Pict in a guarded voice; then swiftly, gazing closely in Kull's face, he said, barely above a whisper:

"Ka nama kaa lajerama!"

Kull started. "Ha! What mean you?"

"Know you not?"

"Nay, the words, are unfamiliar; they are of no language I ever heard—and yet, by Valka!—somewhere—I have heard—"

"Aye," was the Pict's only comment. His eyes swept the room, the study room of the palace. Except for a few tables, a divan or two and great shelves of books of parchment, the room was barren compared to the grandeur of the rest of the palace.

"Tell me, king, who guards the door?"

"Eighteen of the Red Slayers. But how come you, stealing through the gardens by night and scaling the walls of the palace?"

Brule sneered. "The guards of Valusia are blind buffaloes. I could steal their girls from under their noses. I stole amid them and they saw me not nor heard me. And the walls—I could scale them without the aid of vines. I have hunted tigers on the foggy beaches when the sharp east breezes blew the mist in from seaward and I have climbed the steeps of the western sea mountain. But come—nay, touch this armlet."

He held out his arm and, as Kull complied wonderingly, gave an apparent sigh of relief.

"So. Now throw off those kingly robes; for there are ahead of you this night such deeds as no Atlantean ever dreamed of."

Brule himself was clad only in a scanty loin-cloth through which was thrust a short, curved sword.

"And who are you to give me orders?" asked Kull, slightly resentful.

"Did not Ka-nu bid you follow me in all things?" asked the Pict irritably, his eyes flashing momentarily. "I have no love for you, lord, but for the moment I have put the thought of feuds from my mind. Do you likewise. But come."

Walking noiselessly, he led the way across the room to the door. A slide in the door allowed a view of the outer corridor, unseen from without, and the Pict bade Kull look.

"What see you?"

"Naught but the eighteen guardsmen."

The Pict nodded, motioned Kull to follow him across the room. At a panel in the opposite wall Brule stopped and fumbled there a moment. Then with a light movement he stepped back, drawing his sword as he did so. Kull gave an exclamation as the panel swung silently open, revealing a dimly lighted passageway.

"A secret passage!" swore Kull softly. "And I knew nothing of it! By Valka, someone shall dance for this!"

"Silence!" hissed the Pict.

Brule was standing like a bronze statue as if straining every nerve for the slightest sound; something about his attitude made Kull's hair prickle slightly, not from fear but from some eery anticipation. Then beckoning, Brule stepped through the secret doorway which stood open behind them. The passage was bare, but not dust-covered as should have been the case with an unused secret corridor. A vague, gray light filtered through somewhere, but the source of it was not apparent. Every few feet Kull saw doors, invisible, as he knew, from the outside, but easily apparent from within.

"The palace is a very honeycomb," he muttered.

"Aye. Night and day you are watched, king, by many eyes."

The king was impressed by Brule's manner. The Pict went forward slowly, warily, half crouching, blade held low and thrust forward. When he spoke it was in a whisper and he continually flung glances from side to side.

The corridor turned sharply and Brule warily gazed past the turn.

"Look!" he whispered. "But remember! No word! No sound—on your life!"

Kull cautiously gazed past him. The corridor changed just at the bend to a flight of steps. And then Kull recoiled. At the foot of those stairs lay the eighteen Red Slayers who were that night stationed to watch the king's study room. Brule's grip upon his mighty arm and Brule's fierce whisper at his shoulder alone kept Kull from leaping down those stairs.

"Silent, Kull! Silent, in Valka's name!" hissed the Pict. "These corridors are empty now, but I risked much in showing you, that you might then believe what I had to say. Back now to the room of study." And he retraced his steps, Kull following; his mind in a turmoil of bewilderment.

"This is treachery," muttered the king, his steel-gray eyes a-smolder, "foul and swift! Mere minutes have passed since those men stood at guard."

Again in the room of study Brule carefully closed the secret panel and motioned Kull to look again through the slit of the outer door. Kull gasped audibly. For without stood the eighteen guardsmen!

"This is sorcery!" he whispered, half-drawing his sword. "Do dead men guard the king?"

"Aye!" came Brule's scarcely audible reply; there was a strange expression in the Pict's scintillant eyes. They looked squarely into each other's eyes for an instant, Kull's brow wrinkled in a puzzled scowl as he strove to read the Pict's inscrutable face.

Then Brule's lips, barely moving, formed the words: "The—snake—that—speaks!"

"Silent!" whispered Kull, laying his hand over Brule's mouth. "That is death to speak! That is a name accursed!"

The Pict's fearless eyes regarded him steadily.

"Look again, King Kull. Perchance the guard was changed."

"Nay, those are the same men. In Valka's name, this is sorcery—this is insanity! I saw with my own eyes the bodies of those men, not eight minutes agone. Yet there they stand."

Brule stepped back, away from the door, Kull mechanically following.

"Kull, what know ye of the traditions of this race ye rule?"

"Much—and yet, little. Valusia is so old—"

"Aye," Brule's eyes lighted strangely, "we are but barbarians—infants compared to the Seven Empires. Not even they themselves know how old they are. Neither the memory of man nor the annals of the historians reach back far enough to tell us when the first men came up from the sea and built cities on the shore. But Kull, men were not always ruled by men!"

The king started. Their eyes met.

"Aye, there is a legend of my people—"

"And mine!" broke in Brule. "That was before we of the isles were allied with Valusia. Aye, in the reign of Lion-fang, seventh war chief of the Picts, so many years ago no man remembers how many. Across the sea we came, from the isles of the sunset, skirting the shores of Atlantis, and falling upon the beaches of Valusia with fire and sword. Aye, the long white beaches resounded with the clash of spears, and the night was like day from the flame of the burning castles. And the king, the king of Valusia, who died on the red sea sands that dim day—" His voice trailed off; the two stared at each other, neither speaking; then each nodded.

"Ancient is Valusia!" whispered Kull. "The hills of Atlantis and Mu were isles of the sea when Valusia was young."

The night breeze whispered through the open window. Not the free, crisp sea air such as Brule and Kull knew and reveled in, in their land, but a breath like a whisper from the past, laden with musk, scents of forgotten things, breathing secrets that were hoary when the world was young.

The tapestries rustled, and suddenly Kull felt like a naked child before the inscrutable wisdom of the mystic past. Again the sense of unreality swept upon him. At the back of his soul stole dim, gigantic phantoms, whispering monstrous things. He sensed that Brule experienced similar thoughts. The Pict's eyes were fixed upon his face with a fierce intensity. Their glances met. Kull felt warmly a sense of comradeship with this member of an enemy tribe. Like rival leopards turning at bay against hunters, these two savages made common cause against the inhuman powers of antiquity.

Brule again led the way back to the secret door. Silently they entered and silently they proceeded down the dim corridor, taking the opposite direction from that in which they had previously traversed it. After a while the Pict stopped and pressed close to one of the secret doors, bidding Kull look with him through the hidden slot.

"This opens upon a little-used stair which leads to a corridor running past the study-room door."

They gazed, and presently, mounting the stair silently, came a silent shape.

"Tu! Chief councilor!" exclaimed Kull. "By night and with bared dagger! How, what means this, Brule?"

"Murder! And foulest treachery!" hissed Brule. "Nay"—as Kull would have flung the door aside and leaped forth—"we are lost if you meet him here, for more lurk at the foot of those stairs. Come!"

Half running, they darted back along the passage. Back through the secret door Brule led, shutting it carefully behind them, then across the chamber to an opening into a room seldom used. There he swept aside some tapestries in a dim corner nook and, drawing Kull with him, stepped behind them. Minutes dragged. Kull could hear the breeze in the other room blowing the window curtains about, and it seemed to him like the murmur of ghosts. Then through the door, stealthily, came Tu, chief councilor of the king. Evidently he had come through the study room and, finding it empty, sought his victim where he was most likely to be.

He came with upraised dagger, walking silently. A moment he halted, gazing about the apparently empty room, which was lighted dimly by a single candle. Then he advanced cautiously, apparently at a loss to understand the absence of the king. He stood before the hiding place—and—

"Slay!" hissed the Pict.

Kull with a single mighty leap hurled himself into the room. Tu spun, but the blinding, tigerish speed of the attack gave him no chance for defense or counter-attack. Sword steel flashed in the dim light and grated on bone as Tu toppled backward, Kull's sword standing out between his shoulders.

Kull leaned above him, teeth bared in the killer's snarl, heavy brows a-scowl above eyes that were like the gray ice of the cold sea. Then he released the hilt and recoiled, shaken, dizzy, the hand of death at his spine.

For as he watched, Tu's face became strangely dim and unreal; the features mingled and merged in a seemingly impossible manner. Then, like a fading mask of fog, the face suddenly vanished and in its stead gaped and leered a monstrous serpent's head!

"Valka!" gasped Kull, sweat beading his forehead, and again: "Valka!"

Brule leaned forward, face immobile. Yet his glittering eyes mirrored something of Kull's horror.

"Regain your sword, lord king," said he. "There are yet deeds to be done."

Hesitantly Kull set his hand to the hilt. His flesh crawled as he set his foot upon the terror which lay at their feet, and as some jerk of muscular reaction caused the frightful mouth to gape suddenly, he recoiled, weak with nausea. Then, wrathful at himself, he plucked forth his sword and gazed more closely at the nameless thing that had been known as Tu, chief councilor. Save for the reptilian head, the thing was the exact counterpart of a man.

"A man with the head of a snake!" Kull murmured. "This, then, is a priest of the serpent god?"

"Aye. Tu sleeps unknowing. These fiends can take any form they will. That is, they can, by a magic charm or the like, fling a web of sorcery about their faces, as an actor dons a mask, so that they resemble anyone they wish to."

"Then the old legends were true," mused the king; "the grim old tales few dare even whisper, lest they die as blasphemers, are no fantasies. By Valka, I had thought—I had guessed—but it seems beyond the bounds of reality. Ha! The guardsmen outside the door—"

"They too are snake-men. Hold! What would you do?"

"Slay them!" said Kull between his teeth.

"Strike at the skull if at all," said Brule. "Eighteen wait without the door and perhaps a score more in the corridors. Hark ye, king, Ka-nu learned of this plot. His spies have pierced the inmost fastnesses of the snake priests and they brought hints of a plot. Long ago he discovered the secret passageways of the palace, and at his command I studied the map thereof and came here by night to aid you, lest you die as other kings of Valusia have died. I came alone for the reason that to send more would have roused suspicion. Many could not steal into the palace as I did. Some of the foul conspiracy you have seen. Snakemen guard your door, and that one, as Tu, could pass anywhere else in the palace; in the morning, if the priests failed, the real guards would be holding their places again, nothing knowing, nothing remembering; there to take the blame if the priests succeeded. But stay you here while I dispose of this carrion."

So saying, the Pict shouldered the frightful thing stolidly and vanished with it through another secret panel. Kull stood alone, his mind a-whirl. Neophytes of the mighty serpent, how many lurked among his cities? How might he tell the false from the true? Aye, how many of his trusted councilors, his generals, were men? He could be certain—of whom?

The **secret panel** swung inward and Brule entered.

"You were swift."

"Aye!" The warrior stepped forward, eyeing the floor. "There is gore upon the rug. See?"

Kull bent forward; from the corner of his eye he saw a blur of movement, a glint of steel. Like a loosened bow he whipped erect, thrusting upward. The warrior sagged upon the sword, his own clattering to the floor. Even at that instant Kull reflected grimly that it was appropriate that the traitor should meet his death upon the sliding, upward thrust used so much by his race. Then, as Brule slid from the sword to sprawl motionless on the floor, the face began to merge and fade, and as Kull caught his breath, his hair a-prickle, the human features vanished and there the jaws of a great snake gaped hideously, the terrible beady eyes venomous even in death.

"He was a snake priest all the time!" gasped the king. "Valka! what an elaborate plan to throw me off my guard! Ka-nu there, is he a man? Was it Ka-nu to whom I talked in the gardens? Almighty Valka!" as his flesh crawled with a horrid thought; "are the people of Valusia men or are they all serpents?"

Undecided he stood, idly seeing that the thing named Brule no longer wore the dragon armlet. A sound made him wheel.

Brule was coming though the secret door.

"Hold!" upon the arm upthrown to halt the Mug's hovering sword gleamed the dragon armlet. "Valka!" The Pict stopped short. Then a grim smile curled his lips.

"By the gods of the seas! These demons are crafty past reckoning. For it must be that that one lurked in the corridors, and seeing me go carrying the carcass of that other, took my appearance. So. I have another to do away with."

"Hold!" there was the menace of death in Kull's voice; "I have seen two men turn to serpents before my eyes. How may I know if you are a true man?"

Brule laughed. "For two reasons, King Kull. No snake-man wears this"—he indicated the dragon armlet—"nor can any say these words," and again Kull heard the strange phrase: "Ka nama kaa lajerama."

"Ka nama kaa lajerama," Kull repeated mechanically. "Now where, in Valka 's name, have I heard that? I have not! And yet—and yet—"

"Aye, you remember, Kull," said Brule. "Through the dim corridors of memory those words lurk; though you never heard them in this life, yet in the bygone ages they were so terribly impressed upon the soul mind that never dies, that they will always strike dim chords in your memory, though you be reincarnated for a million years to come. For that phrase has come secretly down the grim and bloody eons, since when, uncounted centuries ago, those words were watchwords for the race of men who battled with the grisly beings of the Elder Universe. For none but a real man of men may speak them, whose jaws and mouth are shaped different from any

other creature. Their meaning has been forgotten but not the words themselves."

"True," said Kull. "I remember the legends—Valka!" He stopped short, staring, for suddenly, like the silent swinging wide of a mystic door, misty, unfathomed reaches opened in the recesses of his consciousness and for an instant he seemed to gaze back through the vastnesses that spanned life and life; seeing through the vague and ghostly fogs dim shapes reliving dead centuries—men in combat with hideous monsters, vanquishing a planet of frightful terrors. Against a gray, ever-shifting background moved strange, nightmare forms, fantasies of lunacy and fear; and man, the jest of the gods, the blind, wisdomless striver from dust to dust, following the long bloody trail of his destiny, knowing not why, bestial, blundering, like a great murderous child, yet feeling somewhere a spark of divine fire…. Kull drew a hand across his brow, shaken; these sudden glimpses into the abysses of memory always startled him.

"They are gone," said Brule, as if scanning his secret mind; "the bird-women, the harpies, the bat-men, the flying fiends, the wolf-people, the demons, the goblins—all save such as this being that lies at our feet, and a few of the wolf-men. Long and terrible was the war, lasting through the bloody centuries, since first the first men, risen from the mire of apedom, turned upon those who then ruled the world. And at last mankind conquered, so long ago that naught but dim legends come to us through the ages. The snake-people were the last to go, yet at last men conquered even them and drove them forth into the waste lands of the world, there to mate with true snakes until some day, say the sages, the horrid breed shall vanish utterly. Yet the Things returned in crafty guise as men grew soft and degenerate, forgetting ancient wars. Ah, that was a grim and secret war! Among the men of the Younger Earth stole the frightful monsters of the Elder Planet, safeguarded by their horrid wisdom and mysticisms, taking all forms and shapes, doing deeds of horror secretly. No man knew who was true man and who false. No man could trust any man. Yet by means of their own craft they formed ways by which the false might be known from the true. Men took for a sign and a standard the figure of the flying dragon, the winged dinosaur,

a monster of past ages, which was the greatest foe of the serpent. And men used those words which I spoke to you as a sign and symbol, for as I said, none but a true man can repeat them. So mankind triumphed. Yet again the fiends came after the years of forgetfulness had gone by—for man is still an ape in that he forgets what is not ever before his eyes. As priests they came; and for that men in their luxury and might had by then lost faith in the old religions and worships, the snake-men, in the guise of teachers of a new and truer cult, built a monstrous religion about the worship of the serpent god. Such is their power that it is now death to repeat the old legends of the snake-people, and people bow again to the serpent god in new form; and blind fools that they are, the great hosts of men see no connection between this power and the power men overthrew eons ago. As priests the snake-men are content to rule—and yet—" He stopped.

"Go on." Kull felt an unaccountable stirring of the short hair at the base of his scalp.

"Kings have reigned as true men in Valusia," the Pict whispered, "and yet, slain in battle, have died serpents—as died he who fell beneath the spear of Lion-fang on the red beaches when we of the isles harried the Seven Empires. And how can this be, Lord Kull? These kings were born of women and lived as men! This—the true kings died in secret—as you would have died tonight—and priests of the Serpent reigned in their stead, no man knowing."

Kull cursed between his teeth. "Aye, it must be. No one has ever seen a priest of the Serpent and lived, that is known. They live in utmost secrecy."

"The statecraft of the Seven Empires is a mazy, monstrous thing," said Brule. "There the true men know that among them glide the spies of the serpent, and the men who are the Serpent's allies—such as Kaanuub, baron of Blaal—yet no man dares seek to unmask a suspect lest vengeance befall him. No man trusts his fellow and the true statesmen dare not speak to each other what is in the minds of all. Could they be sure, could a snake-man or plot be unmasked before them all, then would the power of the Serpent be more than half broken; for all would then ally and make common cause, sifting out the traitors. Ka-nu alone is of sufficient shrewdness and courage to cope with them, and even Ka-nu learned only enough of their plot to tell me what would happen—what has happened up to this time. Thus far I was prepared; from now on we must trust to our luck and our craft. Here and now I think we are safe; those snake-men without the door dare not leave their post lest true men come here unexpectedly. But tomorrow they will try something else, you may be sure. Just what they will do, none can say, not even Ka-nu; but we must stay at each other's sides, King Kull, until we conquer or both be dead. Now come with me while I take this carcass to the hiding-place where I took the other being."

Kull followed the Pict with his grisly burden through the secret panel and down the dim corridor. Their feet, trained to the silence of the wilderness, made no noise. Like phantoms they glided through the ghostly light, Kull wondering that the corridors should be deserted; at every turn he expected to run full upon some frightful apparition. Suspicion surged back upon him; was this Pict leading him into ambush? He fell back a pace or two behind Brule, his ready sword hovering at the Pict's unheeding back. Brule should die first if he meant treachery. But if the Pict was aware of the king's suspicion, he showed no sign. Stolidly he tramped along, until they came to a room, dusty and long unused, where moldy tapestries hung heavy. Brule drew aside some of these and concealed the corpse behind them.

Then they turned to retrace their steps, when suddenly Brule halted with such abruptness that he was closer to death than he knew; for Kull's nerves were on edge.

"Something moving in the corridor," hissed the Piet. "Ka-nu said these ways would be empty, yet—"

He drew his sword and stole into the corridor, Kull following warily.

A short way down the corridor a strange, vague glow appeared that came toward them. Nerves a-leap, they waited, backs to the corridor wall; for what they knew not, but Kull heard Brule's breath hiss through his teeth and was reassured as to Brule's loyalty.

The glow merged into a shadowy form. A shape vaguely like a man it was, but misty and illusive, like a wisp of fog, that grew more tangible as it approached, but never fully material. A face looked at them, a pair of luminous great eyes, that seemed to hold all the tortures of a million centuries. There was no menace in that face, with its dim, worn features, but only a great pity—and that face—that face—

"Almighty gods!" breathed Kull, an icy hand at his soul: "Eallal, king of Valusia, who died a thousand years ago!"

Brule shrank back as far as he could, his narrow eyes widened in a blaze of pure horror, the sword shaking in his grip, unnerved for the first time that weird night. Erect and defiant stood Kull, instinctively holding his useless sword at the ready; flesh a-crawl, hair a-prickle, yet still a king of kings, as ready to challenge the powers of the unknown dead as the powers of the living.

The phantom came straight on, giving them no heed; Kull shrank back as it passed them, feeling an icy breath like a breeze from the arctic snow. Straight on went the shape with slow, silent footsteps, as if the chains of all the ages were upon those vague feet; vanishing about a bend of the corridor.

"Valka!" muttered the Pict, wiping the cold beads from his brow; "that was no man! That was a ghost!"

"Aye!" Kull shook his head wonderingly. "Did you not recognize the face? That was Eallal, who reigned in Valusia a thousand years ago and who was found hideously murdered in his throneroom—the room now known as the Accursed Room. Have you not seen his statue in the Fame Room of Kings?"

"Yes, I remember the tale now. Gods, Kull! that is another sign of the frightful and foul power of the snake priests—that king was slain by snake-people and thus his soul became their slave, to do their bidding throughout eternity! For the sages have ever maintained that if a man is slain by a snake-man his ghost becomes their slave."

A shudder shook Kull's gigantic frame. "Valka! But what a fate! Hark ye"—his fingers closed upon Brule's sinewy arm like steel—"hark ye! If I am wounded unto death by these foul monsters, swear that ye will smite your sword through my breast lest my soul be enslaved."

"I swear," answered Brule, his fierce eyes lighting. "And do ye the same by me, Kull."

Their strong right hands met in a silent sealing of their bloody bargain.

4. MASKS

Kull sat upon his throne and gazed broodingly out upon the sea of faces turned toward him. A courtier was speaking in evenly modulated tones, but the king scarcely heard him. Close by, Tu, chief councilor, stood ready at Kull's command, and each time the king looked at him, Kull shuddered inwardly. The surface of court life was as the unrippled surface of the sea between tide and tide. To the musing king the affairs of the night before seemed as a dream, until his eyes dropped to the arm of his throne. A brown, sinewy hand rested there, upon the wrist of which gleamed a dragon armlet; Brule stood beside his throne and ever the Pict's fierce secret whisper brought him back from the realm of unreality in which he moved.

No, that was no dream, that monstrous interlude. As he sat upon his throne in the Hall of Society and gazed upon the courtiers, the ladies, the lords, the statesmen, he seemed to see their faces as things of illusion, things unreal, existent only as shadows and mockeries of substance. Always he had seen their faces as masks but before he had looked on them with contemptuous tolerance, thinking to see beneath the masks shallow, puny souls, avaricious, lustful, deceitful; now there was a grim undertone, a sinister meaning, a vague horror that lurked beneath the smooth masks. While he exchanged courtesies with some nobleman or councilor he seemed to see the smiling face fade like smoke and the frightful jaws of a serpent gaping there. How many of those he looked upon were horrid, inhuman monsters, plotting his death, beneath the smooth mesmeric illusion of a human face?

Valusia—land of dreams and nightmares—a kingdom of the shadows, ruled by phantoms who glided back and forth behind the painted curtains, mocking the futile king who sat upon the throne—himself a shadow.

And like a comrade shadow Brule stood by his side, dark eyes glittering from immobile face. A real man, Brule! And Kull felt his friendship for the savage become a thing of reality and sensed that Brule felt a friendship for him beyond the mere necessity of statecraft.

And what, mused Kull, were the realities of life? Ambition, power, pride? The friendship of man, the love of women—which Kull had never known—Battle, plunder, what? Was it the real Kull who sat upon the throne or was it the real Kull who had sealed the hills of Atlantis, harried the far isles of the sunset, and laughed upon the green roaring tides of the Atlantean sea? How could a man be so many different men in a lifetime? For Kull knew that there were many Kulls and he wondered which was the real Kull. After all, the priests of the Serpent merely went a step further in their magic, for all men wore masks, and many a different mask with each different man or woman; and Kull wondered if a serpent did not lurk under every mask.

So he sat and brooded in strange, mazy thought ways, and the courtiers came and went and the minor affairs of the day were completed, until at last the king and Brule sat alone in the Hall of Society save for the drowsy attendants.

Kull felt a weariness. Neither he nor Brule had slept the night before, nor had Kull slept the night before that, when in the gardens of Ka-nu he had had his first hint of the weird things to be. Last night nothing further had occurred after they had returned to the study room from the secret corridors, but they had neither dared nor cared to sleep. Kull, with the incredible vitality of a wolf, had aforetime gone for days upon days without sleep, in his wild savage days, but now his mind was edged from constant thinking and from the nerve-breaking eeriness of the past night. He needed sleep, but sleep was furthest from his mind.

And he would not have dared sleep if he had thought of it. Another thing that had shaken him was the fact that though he and Brule had kept a close watch to see if, or when, the study-room guard was changed, yet it was changed without their knowledge; for the next morning those who stood on guard were able to repeat the magic words of Brule, but they remembered nothing out of the ordinary. They thought that they had stood at guard all night, as usual, and Kull said nothing to the contrary. He believed them true men, but

Brule had advised absolute secrecy, and Kull also thought it best.

Now Brule leaned over the throne, lowering his voice so not even a lazy attendant could hear: "They will strike soon, I think, Kull. A while ago Ka-nu gave me a secret sign. The priests know that we know of their plot, of course, but they know not how much we know. We must be ready for any sort of action. Ka-nu and the Pictish chiefs will remain within hailing distance now until this is settled one way or another. Ha, Kull, if it comes to a pitched battle, the streets and the castles bf Valusia will run red!"

Kull smiled grimly. He would greet any sort of action with a ferocious joy. This wandering in a labyrinth of illusion and magic was extremely irksome to his nature. He longed for the leap and clang of swords, for the joyous freedom of battle.

Then into the Hall of Society came Tu again, and the rest of the councilors.

"Lord king, the hour of the council is at hand and we stand ready to escort you to the council room."

Kull rose, and the councilors bent the knee as he passed through the way opened by them for his passage, rising behind him and following. Eyebrows were raised as the Pict strode defiantly behind the king, but no one dissented. Brule's challenging gaze swept the smooth faces of the councilors with the defiance of an intruding savage.

The group passed through the halls and came at last to the council chamber. The door was closed, as usual, and the councilors arranged themselves in the order of their rank before the dais upon which stood the king. Like a bronze statue Brule took up his stand behind Kull.

Kull swept the room with a swift stare. Surely no chance of treachery here. Seventeen councilors there were, all known to him; all of them had espoused his cause when he ascended the throne.

"Men of Valusia—" he began in the conventional manner, then halted, perplexed. The councilors had risen as a man and were moving toward him. There was no hostility in their looks, but their actions were strange for a council room. The foremost was close to him when Brule sprang forward, crouched like a leopard.

"Ka nama kaa lajerama!" his voice crackled through the sinister silence of the room and the foremost councilor recoiled, hand flashing to his robes; and like a spring released Brule moved and the man pitched headlong to the glint of his sword—headlong he pitched and lay still while his face faded and became the head of a mighty snake.

"Slay, Kull!" rasped the Pict's voice. "They be all serpent men!"

The rest was a scarlet maze. Kull saw the familiar faces dim like fading fog and in their places gaped horrid reptilian visages as the whole band rushed forward. His mind was dazed but his giant body faltered not.

The singing of his sword filled the room, and the onrushing flood broke in a red wave. But they surged forward again, seemingly willing to fling their lives away in order to drag down the king. Hideous jaws gaped at him; terrible eyes blazed into his unblinkingly; a frightful fetid scent pervaded the atmosphere—the serpent scent that Kull had known in southern jungles. Swords and daggers leaped at him and he was dimly aware that they wounded him. But Kull was in his element; never before had he faced such grim foes but it mattered little; they lived, their veins held blood that could be spilt and they died when his great sword cleft their skulls or drove through their bodies. Slash, thrust, thrust and swung. Yet had Kull died there but for the man who crouched at his side, parrying and thrusting. For the king was clear berserk, fighting in the terrible Atlantean way, that seeks death to deal death; he made no effort to avoid thrusts and slashes, standing straight up and ever plunging forward, no thought in his frenzied mind but to slay. Not often did Kull forget his fighting craft in his primitive fury, but now some chain had broken in his soul, flooding his mind with a red wave of slaughter-lust. He slew a foe at each blow, but they surged about him, and time and again Brule turned a thrust that would have slain, as he crouched beside Kull, parrying and warding with cold skill, slaying not as Kull slew with long slashes and plunges, but with short overhand blows and upward thrusts.

Kull laughed, a laugh of insanity. The frightful faces swirled about him in a scarlet blaze. He felt steel sink into his arm and dropped his sword in a flashing arc that cleft his foe to the breast-bone. Then the mists faded and the king saw that he and Brule stood alone above a sprawl of hideous crimson figures who lay still upon the floor.

"Valka! what a killing!" said Brule, shaking the blood from his eyes. "Kull, had these been warriors who knew how to use the steel, we had died here. These serpent priests know naught of swordcraft and die easier than any men I ever slew. Yet had there been a few more, I think the matter had ended otherwise."

Kull nodded. The wild berserker blaze had passed, leaving a mazed feeling of great weariness. Blood seeped from wounds on breast, shoulder, arm and leg. Brule, himself bleeding from a score of flesh wounds, glanced at him in some concern.

"Lord Kull, let us hasten to have your wounds dressed by the women."

Kull thrust him aside with a drunken sweep of his mighty aim.

"Nay, we'll see this through ere we cease. Go you, though, and have your wounds seen to—I command it."

The Pict laughed grimly. "Your wounds are more than mine, lord king—" he began, then stopped as a sudden thought struck him. "By Valka, Kull, this is not the council room!"

Kull looked about and suddenly other fogs seemed to fade. "Nay, this is the room where Eallal died a thousand years ago—since unused and named 'Accursed.'"

"Then by the gods, they tricked us after all!" exclaimed Brule in a fury, kicking the corpses at their feet. "They caused us to walk like fools into their ambush! By their magic they changed the appearance of all—"

"Then there is further deviltry afoot," said Kull, "for if there be true men in the councils of Valusia they should be in the real council room now. Come swiftly."

And leaving the room with its ghastly keepers they hastened through halls that seemed deserted until they came to the real council room. Then Kull halted with a ghastly shudder. From the council room sounded a voice speaking, and the voice was his!

With a hand that shook he parted the tapestries and gazed into the room. There sat the councilors, counterparts of the men he and Brule had just slain, and upon the dais stood Kull, king of Valnsia.

He stepped back, his mind reeling.

"This is insanity!" he whispered. "Am I Kull? Do I stand here or is that Kull yonder in very truth and am I but a shadow, a figment of thought?"

Brule's hand clutching his shoulder, shaking him fiercely, brought him to his senses.

"Valka's name, be not a fool! Can you yet be astounded after all we have seen? See you not that those are true men bewitched by a snake-man who has taken your form, as those others look their forms? By now you should have been slain and yon monster reigning in your stead, unknown by those who bowed to you. Leap and slay swiftly or else we are undone. The Red Slayers, true men, stand close on each hand and none but you can reach and slay him. Be swift!"

Kull shook off the onrushing dizziness, flung back his head in the old, defiant gesture. He took a long, deep breath as does a strong swimmer before diving into the sea; then, sweeping back the tapestries, made the dais in a single lionlike bound. Brule had spoken truth. There stood men of the Red Slayers, guardsmen trained to move quick as the striking leopard; any but Kull had died ere he could reach the usurper. But the sight of Kull, identical with the man upon the dais, held them in their tracks, their minds stunned for an instant, and that was long enough. He upon the dais snatched for his sword, but even as his fingers closed upon the hilt, Kull's sword stood out behind his shoulders and the thing that men had thought the king pitched forward from the dais to lie silent upon the floor.

"Hold!" Kull's lifted hand and kingly voice stopped the rush that had started, and while they stood astounded he pointed to the thing which lay before them—whose face was fading into that of a snake. They recoiled, and from one door came Brule and from another came Ka-nu.

These grasped the king's bloody hand and Ka-nu spoke: "Men of Valusia, you have seen with your own eyes. This is the true Kull, the mightiest king to whom Valusia has ever bowed. The power of the

Serpent is broken and ye be all true men. King Kull, have you commands?"

"Lift that carrion," said Kull, and men of the guard took up the thing.

"Now follow me," said the king, and he made his way to the Accursed Room. Brule, with a look of concern, offered the support of his arm but Kull shook him off.

The distance seemed endless to the bleeding king, but at last he stood at the door and laughed fiercely and grimly when he heard the horrified ejaculations of the councilors.

At his orders the guardsmen flung the corpse they carried beside the others, and motioning all from the room Kull stepped out last and closed the door.

A wave of dizziness left him shaken. The faces turned to him, pallid and wonderingly, swirled and mingled in a ghostly fog. He felt the blood from his wound trickling down his limbs and he knew that what he was to do, he must do quickly or not at all.

His sword rasped from its sheath.

"Brule, are you there?"

"Aye!" Brule's face looked at him through the mist, close to his shoulder, but Brule's voice sounded leagues and eons away.

"Remember our vow, Brule. And now, bid them stand back."

His left arm cleared a space as he flung up his sword. Then with all his waning power he drove it through the door into the jamb, driving the great sword to the hilt and sealing the room forever.

Legs braced wide, he swayed drunkenly, facing the horrified councilors. "Let this room be doubly accursed. And let those rotting skeletons lie there forever as a sign of the dying might of the serpent. Here I swear that I shall hunt the serpent-men from land to land, from sea to sea, giving no rest until all be slain, that good triumph and the power of Hell be broken. This thing I swear—I—Kull—king—of—Valusia."

His knees buckled as the faces swayed and swirled. The councilors leaped forward, but ere they could reach him, Kull slumped to the floor, and lay still, face upward.

The councilors surged about the fallen king, chattering and shrieking. Ka-nu beat them back with his clenched fists, cursing savagely.

"Back, you fools! Would you stifle the little life that is yet in him? How, Brule, is he dead or will he live?"—to the warrior who bent above the prostrate Kull.

"Dead?" sneered Brule irritably. "Such a man as this is not so easily killed. Lack of sleep and loss of blood have weakened him—by Valka, he has a score of deep wounds, but none of them mortal. Yet have those gibbering fools bring the court women here at once."

Brule's eyes lighted with a fierce, proud light.

"Valka, Ka-nu, but here is such a man as I knew not existed in these degenerate days. He will be in the saddle in a few scant days and then may the serpent-men of the world beware of Kull of Valusia. Valka! but that will be a rare hunt! Ah, I see long years of prosperity for the world with such a king upon the throne of Valusia."

**The first Kull of Atlantis story, set in Howard's Thurian Age.
Originally published in Weird Tales, Volume 14 Issue 2 (Aug. 1929)**

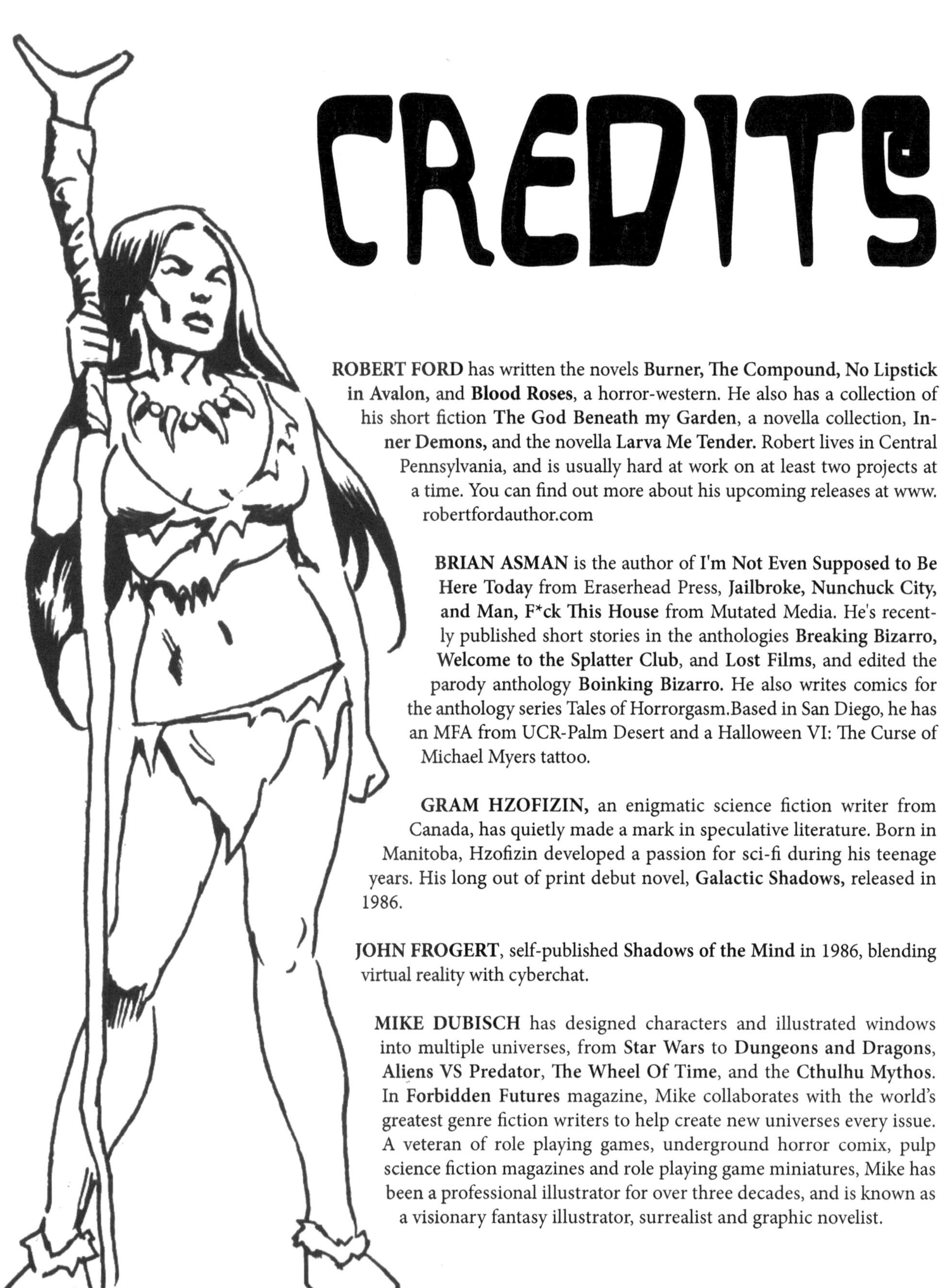

CREDITS

ROBERT FORD has written the novels **Burner, The Compound, No Lipstick in Avalon,** and **Blood Roses,** a horror-western. He also has a collection of his short fiction **The God Beneath my Garden,** a novella collection, **Inner Demons,** and the novella **Larva Me Tender.** Robert lives in Central Pennsylvania, and is usually hard at work on at least two projects at a time. You can find out more about his upcoming releases at www.robertfordauthor.com

BRIAN ASMAN is the author of **I'm Not Even Supposed to Be Here Today** from Eraserhead Press, **Jailbroke, Nunchuck City, and Man, F*ck This House** from Mutated Media. He's recently published short stories in the anthologies **Breaking Bizarro, Welcome to the Splatter Club,** and **Lost Films,** and edited the parody anthology **Boinking Bizarro.** He also writes comics for the anthology series Tales of Horrorgasm.Based in San Diego, he has an MFA from UCR-Palm Desert and a Halloween VI: The Curse of Michael Myers tattoo.

GRAM HZOFIZIN, an enigmatic science fiction writer from Canada, has quietly made a mark in speculative literature. Born in Manitoba, Hzofizin developed a passion for sci-fi during his teenage years. His long out of print debut novel, **Galactic Shadows,** released in 1986.

JOHN FROGERT, self-published **Shadows of the Mind** in 1986, blending virtual reality with cyberchat.

MIKE DUBISCH has designed characters and illustrated windows into multiple universes, from **Star Wars** to **Dungeons and Dragons, Aliens VS Predator, The Wheel Of Time,** and the **Cthulhu Mythos.** In **Forbidden Futures** magazine, Mike collaborates with the world's greatest genre fiction writers to help create new universes every issue. A veteran of role playing games, underground horror comix, pulp science fiction magazines and role playing game miniatures, Mike has been a professional illustrator for over three decades, and is known as a visionary fantasy illustrator, surrealist and graphic novelist.

ROBERT E. HOWARD (1906-1936) was a prolific American writer widely recognized for his significant contributions to the sword and sorcery genre. Howard was born in Peaster, Texas, and developed an early passion for history and storytelling. He began his writing career in the 1920s, achieving fame for creating the iconic character Conan the Barbarian, first appearing in **Weird Tales** magazine in 1932. Howard's Conan stories, set in the mythical Hyborian Age, were characterized by vivid descriptions, fast-paced action, and a rugged, brooding protagonist. Apart from Conan, Howard created other memorable characters like King Kull and Solomon Kane, expanding his influence in fantasy literature. His writing style, marked by a robust, visceral narrative voice, significantly shaped modern fantasy and inspired generations of writers and readers. Tragically, Howard's life was cut short at the age of 30. Still, his legacy endures through his vast body of work, which continues to be celebrated for its imagination, intensity, and influence on the fantasy genre.

CODY GOODFELLOW has written nine novels and five collections of short stories. His writing has been favored with three Wonderland Book Awards. His comics work has been featured in **Mystery Meat, Creepy, Slow Death Zero** and **Skin Crawl**. As an actor, he has appeared in numerous short films, TV shows, music videos by Anthrax and Beck, and a Days Inn commercial. He also wrote, co-produced and scored the Lovecraftian hygiene films **Baby Got Bass** and **Stay At Home Dad**, which can be viewed on YouTube. He lives in San Diego, California.

SAM RICHARD is the author of **Sabbath of the Fox-Devils** and the Wonderland Award-Winning Collection **To Wallow in Ash & Other Sorrows**. The owner of Weirdpunk Books, he has edited and co-edited several anthologies, including the Splatterpunk Award-Nominated **The New Flesh: A Literary Tribute to David Cronenberg, Zombie Punks Fuck Off, and Beautiful/Grotesque.** Widowed in 2017, he slowly rots in Minneapolis with his dog, Nero.

ISMAEL GALVAN is a Chicano writer and illustrator from North County San Diego. He is the co-creator of the Tamale Guy comic series. His work has appreared in **Forbidden Futures**. He is also the author **Hidden in the Thorns**, a short story collection of speculative fiction. Besides making art, Ish teaches art classes on comic book history and creation to young students.

MATTHEW MEDNEY, A Prolific Writer" (Variety) with the ultimate goal of looking to expand minds and engage readers through high concept Science Fiction, Medney the former CEO of **Heavy Metal Magazine** has authored best selling works such as his hard sci-fi novel **Beyond Kuiper: The Galactic Star Alliance, Above The Ground** and the graphic novel **Dark Wing**. In addition, he has penned multiple comic books including **The Red, Stable, Remnant** and his highly anticipated forthcoming work **The Adventures of Adrienne James**, which can best be described as "female Indiana Jones - in space" - SYFY Other notable comic and graphic novel works Medney has helmed include work done in collaboration with bands and music festivals such as the largest Hip Hop Festival in the world Rolling Loud, Grammy award winning musician Shaggy, along with other notable talents such as Floyd Mayweather Jr. NGHTMRE, K?D, Insomniac's Events Project Z, Imagine Music Festival, Disney and the NFL. In addition to his graphic novel work, Medney is the Head Writer for web3 juggernaut **Star Atlas**. An AAA MMO Unreal 5 video game, Star Atlas, has raised more than 300 million dollars to create the vision of the future in gaming. For television and film, Medney is repped by the Gotham Group and has several films in development at various stages and studios currently.

PAT SMILET, a first-time sci-fi author from Cleveland, who has passion for futuristic worlds and space operas..